The
Tide Turner

'An exciting, well-written fantasy, it gives us the pleasurable shock of seeing life from an unexpected angle.'   Amanda Craig, *The Times*

'gorgeous undersea descriptions'   *Telegraph*

'a wonderful underwater journey filled with threat and excitement . . . a fresh and vivid undersea adventure that is richly plotted and amazingly realistic.'   *South China Morning Post*

The Tide Turner

ANGELA MCALLISTER

Illustrated by Peter Bailey

Orion
Children's Books

With grateful thanks to the Society of Authors
for their generous grant and advice over many years

First published in Great Britain in 2006
by Orion Children's Books
This paperback edition published in 2007
by Orion Children's Books
a division of the Orion Publishing Group Ltd
Orion House
5 Upper St Martin's Lane
London WC2H 9EA
An Hachette Livre UK Company

1 3 5 7 9 10 8 6 4 2

The Orion Publishing Group's policy is to use papers that
are natural, renewable and recyclable products and made
from wood grown in sustainable forests. The logging and
manufacturing processes are expected to conform to the
environmental regulations of the country of origin.

A catalogue record for this book is
available from the British Library

Printed in Great Britain by
Clays Ltd, St Ives plc

ISBN 978 1 84255 562 0
www.orionbooks.co.uk

For Susie

Contents

One

Cal

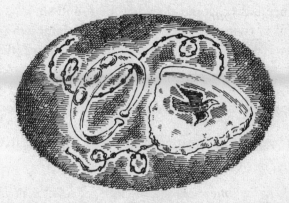

Cal lay awake, watching for the first light of dawn. Her heart beat furiously inside her chest like a wild thing in a cage.

All through the long night she'd tossed on restless tides of sleep and tumbled in an undertow of turbulent dreams. Now, at last, a dim light shimmered on the stone windowsill.

Night was over.

Cal rose quickly and sat on her bed. She ran her fingers through the tangles of her copper hair and peered around the room. She could see little, but Cal had always lived in the half-dark. A world of shadow she now made ready to escape.

She reached for the earthenware jug standing on the floor by the bed, tipped it carefully and thrust her arm inside, pulling out a fistful of knotted twine. Cal worried about what her father would do when he found she'd gone. The handful of twine was her message, explaining why she had to leave. But would he understand? Cal remembered his recent words, 'I love you more than breath itself, little spinner,' and she knew it was true. But how could you really love someone and keep secrets; secrets that hurt so much?

'I will come back,' Cal insisted silently to herself. 'It's not for ever, but I have to go.'

On an upturned crate beside the bed was a large shell bowl containing Cal's treasures. Her fingers found a bronze bracelet with three amber beads. Hurriedly she slipped it onto her wrist. There too was a tiny tarnished spoon and a bone comb. Her father had bargained for them with a trader. They were pretty enough but not what she was looking for. She took out a fragment of pottery. On the rim a painted bird was flying in a smudge of blue sky. Cal put her thumb on the bird's body, as she had done many times before, and felt the slight indentation of the potter's thumbprint, only a little bigger than her own. She put the wedge of broken clay into a small woven bag, surprised at how important these touchstones suddenly seemed, now that she was about to leave everything familiar behind.

Nothing will be the same again, she thought and felt a tremor of fear and excitement. Whatever she might discover in the days ahead, Cal was certain she would return changed somehow.

Last she picked out a triangular shard of mirror glass and took it to the window. Although it was badly scratched and the light still weak, Cal could make out a scrap of her reflection: a narrow green eye with red lashes, a scatter of freckles on her creamy cheek and the side of her long nose. She pursed her lips.

'No, I want to see all of me,' she said in a low voice, 'not just a part any more. I need to know who I am, where I came from. If Father won't tell me I'll find out for myself.'

Cal tightened the drawstring bag and fixed it to a plaited belt around her waist, then reached instinctively to her throat for the crystal teardrop pendant she always wore. It had belonged to her mother. She paused, curling her fingers around the pendant in the very place her mother's fingers must have held it, imagining a tiny pulse flowing from one hand to the other. Passing through the absence between them. Pulsing from heart to heart. What more did they share? Cal had to find out. Did her mother have the same russet hair with its curious glints of silver? Did she have Cal's rare skill with injured creatures? Was her mind constantly restless with questions? Cal was certain there must be somebody, somewhere, who could tell her. Someone who could remember what her father found too painful to recall.

Cal took one last look round her room. Under the bed was a plain, wooden box. This had belonged to her mother too, but it was locked and neither Cal nor Pelin, her father, had ever found a key. She sighed. If only it were smaller she would take it.

'No,' she told herself firmly, 'I won't be locked out any more. I'll find my own key.'

Turning her back on the box she began to move silently along the passage towards her father's room.

Pelin lay asleep, with his back to the doorway. Cal gazed at him. She remembered the times she'd slept there as a child, folded in his arms. On those nights, when she had cried for her mother, he'd held her close and the spell of his whispered words had comforted her. Now Cal was older, she had learnt to cry to herself. She didn't want his comfort or protection. It stifled her, imprisoned her.

Pelin muttered restlessly. Cal's eyes prickled. She chewed her lip. For all her resolve she hated to hurt him. She didn't dare go into his room to even whisper goodbye for fear of waking him. Quickly she turned away and slipped down the staircase and across the hall.

Early light dappled the flagstones. She hesitated, clutching the little bag hanging from her belt, and steadied her nerve. Suddenly Cal sensed she was not alone. She spun round . . . Pelin appeared at the top of the stairs.

'Where are you going? It's so early.' He looked confused.

Cal wasn't prepared for this. Now she would have to lie. 'I'm going to the Overbreath. I couldn't sleep.'

'But you can't go alone,' said Pelin, yawning and descending the stairs. 'Let's eat first and then I'll come with you.'

Cal moved nearer the threshold. 'I can go alone, Father, all the others my age do.'

'I don't care what the others do, Calypsia.' Pelin's voice sharpened. 'You're not like them.'

Cal sighed. How many times had she heard those words before? They were always the beginning of an exasperating exchange that went nowhere. Still, she couldn't stop herself from asking, 'Why aren't I like the others?'

Pelin didn't answer. He reached for a stone bench, draped in sealskin, and sank down upon it. Leaning forward, he rested his head in his hands.

'What does that mean, "not like the others"?' Cal persisted.

'It's not safe for you,' said Pelin. 'I'm afraid that – that there are—'

'*What* are you afraid of?' Cal interrupted. 'You must tell me.'

'I can't say. You have to trust me. It's not safe.'

'No!' Cal snapped. 'I *am* old enough. You must trust *me* now.'

Pelin knew she was right. Cal wasn't a child any more. She needed the fingers of his hand along with her own to count the times they'd watched the Great Migration. And how long before she stopped reaching out for his hand? He'd been a fool over-protecting her. Pelin was seized with panic at the thought of letting her go. He wasn't ready.

He couldn't let her slip away like this – hadn't prepared her for what might be waiting, out there, beyond his watchful eye . . .

'I promised your mother,' he said softly.

Cal felt her throat tighten. A shaft of light slipped through the window and sliced across the hall, trembling between father and daughter. Neither spoke.

Why now? Cal thought. When I am just about to go? Then she dared hope. Maybe he is ready to speak, maybe I won't have to go at all.

When Cal was little she had often asked when her mother, Sylla, would come home. But Pelin had always avoided answering her questions, promising to tell her one day – a day that never arrived. Cal's young mind had been unable to grasp that there might be leaving without a return. She would arrange her playthings, hoping to please Sylla when she came back, quizzing her father about when it would be. She made gifts for her mother, threading beads and collecting stones. Then, one evening, she caught Pelin wiping tears from his eyes as he watched her and, without words, she understood what he could never tell her.

Something of the darkness Cal felt inside that night had never left her. From then on she learnt not to upset her father with questions, although it hurt not to ask. But now, maybe this was a chance to coax some memory from him.

Cal moved towards her father. Gently she pulled his hands away from his face.

'What did you promise my mother?' she asked.

Pelin struggled. He had made a promise to Sylla when she told him she was dying. If he broke it he would lose faith with her. It was unthinkable. Yet if he didn't break it and tell their daughter now of the danger she might face how could he protect her? Hadn't he promised to do that too?

But that was not all that troubled him. There were other secrets – deeper secrets overheard, words he had tried to forget, knowledge so burdensome it was almost unbearable . . .

'Help me,' Pelin gasped. His voice sounded strange to Cal. She knew at once his words were not spoken to her.

Cal watched her father sink his head once more upon his hands.

'Tell me,' she shouted desperately. 'I have a right to know! Tell me something! Tell me!'

But Pelin did not look up. Cal cried out in frustration and turned away from him, towards whatever lay beyond. Her tail flashed dangerously as she passed through the rippling curtain of light. Without glancing back she swam off through the sunken village.

Two

Jake

Jake sat in his boat, staring from the sea to the humpback cliffs that rose from the water like the body of a great stone serpent. Glints of ocean light reflected in his grey-blue eyes. A breeze scuffed the water, ruffling his black corkscrew curls. Jake turned, roused by the sharp air that stung his face, and winced at the reminder of how, so recently, his cheeks had stung with tears.

He fingered a nugget of sea glass in his pocket. It had belonged to his father, Charley, who'd kept it in a battered old tobacco tin with his own mother's wedding ring and her gold locket. Charley had shown them all to Jake once, in secret.

'If anything happens to me,' he'd said, puffing as he

hurried to twist the stubborn lid off the tin before his wife, Lil, came home, 'if anything ever happens to me, you sell these, lad. Sell them for Lil.'

But Lil had never needed what little money Charley's keepsakes might have fetched. He and Jake had found her one evening, on their return from a fishing trip, sleeping all wrong in her chair with the fire cold.

'Taking the long rest,' Charley had called it.

That was a year ago. And now Charley, who'd been lost as flotsam without her, was taking the long rest too.

After Charley's funeral Jake had found the tobacco tin, but it didn't feel right to touch the ring and the locket inside – they were for blood family and Jake wasn't blood family, although Charley and Lil were the only kin he knew. He'd just taken the piece of blue glass. It must have meant something to Charley.

The boat pitched. Jake lurched forward and pulled in the oars. That boat was all he'd had when Charley and Lil took him in and all he was left with since they'd gone.

He gazed back at the shore, to the stretch of beach where Charley said he'd found Jake one morning, twelve years ago. It had been a cold, grey day. Sky and sea had dissolved into one another. The lone rowing boat lay on the winter beach. Charley had been taking his usual walk, stumbling along the water's edge, picking through the driftwood, spitting curses at the spray. He stooped to stab at the wet pebbles, picked up a scrap of twine and stuffed it in his pocket, mumbling as he straightened up against the wind.

Suddenly the familiar cry of seabirds was pierced by a shriek. Charley narrowed his eyes and listened. At first he thought it was a whistling gull playing tricks on his ears.

9

But the cry was followed by a desperate bleating that chilled his heart. This time Charley recognised the sound.

He clambered across the stony beach towards the boat. When he saw what was inside he stepped back and crossed himself.

No one ever knew how long the child had been crying in that boat, or how Charley managed to carry a tiny baby, wrapped inside his coat, up the steep cliff steps and along the coast path to the cottage hospital hunched like a white gull on the hillside.

Charley had wanted to leave the baby on the doorstep of the hospital and be gone. Superstition was strong in those parts. Everyone knew the saying: 'Take a child from a salty crib and cry a sea of tears.'

There were many tales about babies found abandoned at the water's edge: restless, moody children who brought tragedy to the families that took them in – most often death by drowning; sad children with unspoken longings who disappeared when a tide was unusually high; feral creatures who haunted the cliffs and caves; children who grew webbed feet . . .

Sea foundlings were feared.

But Charley couldn't leave the baby on the step because he had nothing to wrap it in. 'And I wasn't going to give up my coat,' he told Jake many times later. 'There was a chill wind up there and you were pale as death. So I took you inside. But those nurses could smell the brine on you. They guessed where you'd come from, I saw it in their eyes. Not one would take you from my arms. I had to bring you home to Lil, and she washed you and wrapped you up with a dry sprig of lavender, looked me straight in the eye and said, "That's that, then." '

Lil named the baby Jake after her father and was soon busy fussing over the child. But Charley couldn't get the sound of that baby's cry out of his head. It echoed on the wind and the roar of the waves. And it troubled him. It troubled him that Lil would give her heart to the boy.

A wave slapped the side of the boat. Jake loved the sound of that hollow smack, the hearty way the sea claimed the boat. No one had come for it after Jake was found, so Charley had kept it. When Jake was barely old enough to descend the cliff steps, half jumping, half stumbling, Charley took him down to the beach, bundled him into the old boat and began to teach him how to handle it. Jake loved those hours on the water with Charley. He soon grew confident and was keen to learn anything Charley could teach him.

'Sea born . . .' Charley would say and Jake never questioned this odd remark, but he noticed the silence that always followed, as if there was something left unsaid.

Charley lived just long enough to see Jake master his boat. The week before he died he made a bother about the way Jake was painting it.

'She'll only have one master,' said Jake, pushing the hair from his brow with a paint-smeared hand. 'Who's it going to be?'

Charley grinned and Jake grinned back.

'When the paint's dry you can climb aboard, old man,' said Jake, 'and I'll show you how to catch a crab!' He got a clip round the ear for his cheek, but the following day he and Charley had their last trip together.

Jake had grown strong and wise enough to sail alone. And alone he stood in the chapel when they blessed the coffin of old Charley, who wasn't afraid of the foundling.

Now Jake was left to brood on the sense of it all. There on the water, looking back from a distance, he could make sense of most things: of the river that flowed from the hills, cleaving the rock to the sea; of the steep town that clung to both sides of the valley, spilling its fishermen into their boats; of the harbour arms that kept safe water for their return. He understood the sense of Charley and Lil and their place in the ebb and flow of the town, of their own tides of work and rest. But the sense of himself, that was something Jake had never been able to grasp. Where did he fit in? Why didn't he understand his place, why was nothing about himself clear in his mind's eye? It was only on the boat that his restlessness ceased, dissolving into the dipping, rising rhythm of the waves. The sea always lulled his questions away.

Three

At Sea

Jake turned his gaze away from the land and his thoughts to fishing. Sky and sea had muddled together. Even Jake's sharp eye couldn't make out where one ended and the other began. He'd packed some food and left home early, dressed for the morning cold. Now he stood up, stiff and yawning, and tugged his jumper over his head. He noticed something bob in the water a few yards off. It moved towards him and spun around. Jake looked again. It was the head of a girl – a girl with red hair swirling around her shoulders. She saw Jake and stared, as if paralysed, like a night creature caught in a beam of torchlight. Jake gaped. A shiver of shock ran through his body. He knew this girl.

He'd seen her before – those green eyes, narrow as blades of willow, he'd know them anywhere.

The girl put her head to one side and scowled. Then she disappeared beneath the water with a splash.

Jake blushed, suddenly feeling awkward, alone with her, way out from shore. He'd always kept away from girls at school, but there was something bold about this one he liked. Must be a strong swimmer, he thought, to be so far out. How come he'd never seen her in town? They didn't get many visitors at that time of year, not swimmers like her . . .

Suddenly she appeared, rising with the swell beside the boat and then, as if teasing him, swam underneath and emerged on the other side.

'What's your name?' she asked, tipping her head slightly towards him to catch his reply. Jake noticed a quiver in her voice, almost as if she were singing and speaking at once. He hesitated. After the silent days since Charley's funeral her simple question took him by surprise.

'Jake,' he said. The girl squinted. He repeated his name, a little louder. 'Jake. What's yours?' He couldn't quite bring himself to look her in the eye.

'Cal.'

'You're a long way out.' Jake sat down and fiddled with his fishing rod, pretending to be busy. The girl weaved back and forth a little way off, watching him.

What's she doing here? Jake wondered. She seemed to be alone. There was no one else in the water and he hadn't seen anybody waiting around on the beach. It was a long swim back to shore – Jake knew he couldn't manage it from there, even if the water was calm.

The girl swam up and gripped the side of the boat. It reeled hard and Jake almost lost his balance.

'Cold day for a swim,' he said, steadying himself. He picked up a net and ran it through his fingers. She smiled and shrugged.

Now he noticed the grey sky darken. Jake smelt rain in the air. That's odd, he thought, there'd been no warning of it. Then, as if a silent curse had been uttered, the mood of the sea changed. It heaved and shuddered, shaking up choppy waves that began to slap the boat about. The breeze quickly became a blustery squall.

The girl disappeared beneath the water and then broke through by the stern.

'I wouldn't stay out long in this,' said Jake. He cast an eye at the flinty sky. 'The weather's up to something. Reckon I'll get back. Shall I – do you want to climb in?' But Cal shook her head.

'I can't.' Her voice was almost lost on the wind. The sea rocked about her, spitting crests of pearly foam into the air.

'Why not?' said Jake, growing alarmed as a shroud of threatening cloud tumbled towards them. He had never known the bay turn rough so fast. Thunder growled. Then rain fell, sudden and hard. 'Come on, grab this . . .' He swung out an oar. Once more the girl shook her head, then to Jake's astonishment she plunged beneath the water again. Jake scrambled from one side of the slippery boat to the other, searching for a glimpse of her. It wasn't safe in the water – *where was she?* He kicked off his trainers, ready to dive in, but her coppery head was nowhere to be seen. The sea churned around the boat and spun it like a leaf in a gutter.

'Hey!' Jake shouted, tumbling off balance. He gripped the rowlock and pulled himself up. The sky of rain made one water with the sea. He had to find her . . .

Lightning stabbed the waves. They flashed for a moment like molten foil. There she was, thrusting her thin white arms out to him – just beyond his reach.

'I'm coming!' he shouted. Jake stood to dive just as a huge swell tipped the boat over and threw him into the whirlpool. With an almighty crack the boat crashed on top of him, splinters of timber exploded in all directions. Jake was dragged down. Something smashed into his ankle, pain shot through his leg. Then he blacked out.

Four

Cave

Jake came to in eerie green light, propped against a rocky wall. His head ached. His nose and mouth were full of water.

I'm dead. This is what it feels like to be drowned.

For a while this overwhelming thought obliterated any other. He struggled to think more clearly. He couldn't have died. He was young, he hadn't done anything yet. Jake shut his eyes and fought the waves of nausea that clouded his mind. With tremendous effort, he started to remember – a wild storm and the boat smashing around him; the spinning water sucking him down . . .

He opened his eyes. There was a low roof above his head

and a patch of brightness beyond it. His ankle was sore and his legs stiff with cramp. 'You don't hurt when you're dead,' he told himself, hoping sense might order itself around this one sure fact. 'But if I'm not dead why aren't I choking?' He couldn't understand why he didn't feel the need to take a breath; it was as if the breath inside his lungs was sufficient. 'I'm not drowned . . . but I'm not breathing . . .'

A dark shape moved at the cave mouth. At once Jake recognised the silhouette of the girl. He started, cracked his head on the ledge of rock and cried out. The pain was real, all right. The girl twisted round.

'What's that?' she said, as if startled to hear his voice.

'Where am I?' Jake groaned. 'What happened?'

Cal moved out from behind a rock. In an instant Jake saw her tail. From the waist down she had the body of a dolphin, smooth and silver grey.

'I am dead!'

'No,' said Cal, 'you're not dead.' Her musical voice was clearer through the water than it had been beside his boat. 'If you were dead you wouldn't be talking to me.'

With a beat of her tail she glided towards him, arms at her side. Her strong, supple body moved sinuously, tiny fishes trailing behind her. Once more Jake recognised her green willow eyes, but as she came close he was startled by her fingers – between each was a film of transparent skin. She had webbed hands.

'How can you talk to me?' Cal asked slowly. She studied him, as puzzled by Jake as he was by her. 'How can you speak my language?'

'I – I can't – I don't know,' he stuttered. 'You spoke to me first – up there.'

Cal frowned but didn't answer. It was true. She had watched Creepers like him several times, close enough to hear their voices – but those shrill, sharp sounds had never made any sense to her before.

Cal didn't understand what was happening. At first she hadn't doubted he was dead. But as she'd pushed the broken timber from his body, to look closer, to touch his strange limbs, the Creeper's eyelids had flickered. So Cal had carried him into the cave. And now. . .she was afraid. What had she done?

She swam back to the mouth of the cave and continued searching for the little bag and the bracelet that had been torn from her by the freak whirlpool. All her treasures were lost except the pendant, which had been caught up in her hair but luckily remained fastened around her neck.

As soon as her back was turned, a conger eel slipped out of the shadows and snaked across the sandy cave floor towards Jake. He shuddered. He had seen monsters like these, prize catches on the quay – seen their vicious teeth. He drew back against the wall. The eel swam closer. It slid up and down the  Conger Eel length of his body, pausing to press its repulsive flesh against his shoulder. Cut deep into its cheek was a pink v-shaped scar.

Sensing his distress Cal turned. In a flash she picked up a rock and threw it. The eel jackknifed angrily. It fled to the mouth of the cave, turned to bare its teeth and slithered away.

'Never trust eels,' she said.

Jake's ankle was throbbing. He reached down and flinched as his fingers found a splinter of wood jammed above the bone. Gritting his teeth, he tried to grip the stub end. It took a couple of goes to pull it out and made him retch.

Cal returned to his side but suddenly something made her swing round.

'Ssh!' She froze, listening hard. 'I can hear someone coming. No – there are two of them – three.' Cal curled herself against the wall beside Jake. 'Don't move.' Jake peered into the water. Sure enough, moments later, three shapes emerged from the soupy distance and seemed to be coming towards the cave. Cal pulled herself closer to the rock and as she did her fluke knocked against Jake's ankle. He shoved his fist into his mouth to stop himself from crying out.

The shapes became distinct. To his horror Jake saw that one was a huge blue marlin, with a vicious-looking snout over half the length of its muscular body. The other two were creatures like Cal herself – at least their lower bodies had the dolphin tail but there the likeness ended. These were two young males. Their skin was the blue-black colour of mussel shell and their flanks were notched with identical patterns of chevron scars. Unlike Cal, they had fins on their backs, tipped with a splash of scarlet. Both had jet hair plaited into long, thin rat-tails and each carried a spear. They scowled as they swam, with the marlin between them.

'Bloodfin!' Cal gasped. Was this what her father had tried to warn her about?

One of the Bloodfin slowed before the cave. He swayed, staring at the base of a rock, and gestured to the other to keep a distance. Then, suddenly, he stabbed with his spear, raising a cloud of sand. When the sand settled there was a small squid on the end of the blade. He offered the squid to the marlin, who devoured it in a gulp. The other Bloodfin joined him. They scouted about, seeming to search for something in the water.

'They didn't come this way,' said the oldest-looking Bloodfin. 'But there's Silvertail close, I can smell them.' He swiped at the marlin with his spear. The big fish reared back, then edged closer again and prodded the Bloodfin's tail with the tip of his snout.

The Bloodfin cursed and twisted round.

'One cut and you're sharkmeat!' He grabbed the hilt of a dagger hanging at his knotted belt. 'Why did you have to go off? We'll never find the rest. If we miss the raid we *all* miss the pickings . . .'

'Give him the stuff, Leaper,' said the younger Bloodfin. 'Keep him sweet. We need him.'

Leaper produced a pouch studded with shark fangs. He pulled out a handful of something and flung his fist into the water, releasing hundreds of small red beads.

'Wreek eggs,' whispered Cal. 'All the Lin go mad for them.' Sure enough the marlin writhed about furiously to catch each one, thrashing the water with its tail. The Bloodfin grinned. When the marlin had chased every last egg in the water it returned to its masters and tried to nuzzle up to the pouch.

'Get off!' snarled Leaper. 'You've got to earn this.'

The marlin moved away, but didn't take its eyes off the pouch.

'Bait thinks the Lin are going to give us trouble,' said the younger Bloodfin, 'but Reefer says they're just spears with muscle!'

Leaper grabbed him by the hair and yanked him close. 'Muscle *and* brain,' he whispered fiercely. 'Never forget that, Barb. Muscle and brain.' He let him go. 'Come on. Let's find the others.'

In an instant all three were gone.

'Who were they?' stuttered Jake.

'Bloodfin,' replied Cal, looking after them, 'from the Melt – cold waters far away. I've never seen any before. They're hunters, not farmers like us. Something's wrong. They shouldn't be here.'

'So who are you?' asked Jake. 'What are you? Ouch!'

A spasm of pain gripped his ankle. He reached down to it. Cal gently pushed his fingers aside and examined the wound. Then she took his other ankle in her broad, webbed hands and studied his foot, pinching his toes and heel, prodding his knee. Jake was amazed at her boldness. He wanted to touch her tail but he didn't dare. Close up she looked younger than he was. He noticed her strong, muscular shoulders and arms, and the pearly-grey sheen of her fluke.

'Can you swim with those – those . . .'

'Feet!' he said, not sure whether to feel proud or ashamed of them. Cal looked at him blankly. 'Never mind about my ankle. I can make it out of here.' Jake grabbed the rock, but didn't have the strength to lift himself to his feet. With a groan he collapsed against the wall once more. 'What if those Bloodfin come back? What would they do to us?'

Cal didn't answer. She wasn't prepared for this. She had to think fast. When she'd left home that morning she'd given herself up to the sea, allowed the current to take her where it pleased. To Cal's astonishment it had carried her into the bay, to this boy – this very boy she had secretly watched before. She knew it was more than coincidence. Then the storm had brought them both below, and now, here he was, alive, speaking in her tongue. She had an uneasy feeling that her visits to the Overbreath had breached a threshold, between his world and hers, somehow. That she was responsible.

Cal sighed. She'd waited so long to be free, to search for knowledge of her mother. But she couldn't just abandon this Creeper boy and go on alone. And now there were Bloodfin in her homewaters. Everything was suddenly so strange.

'What happens if they come back?' repeated Jake, weary from the deep ache rising up his leg.

Cal drummed her fist against her side. It was no good. She had no choice now. 'We'll get away,' she said. 'I'll have to take you to my father.' Her plan had been ruined. She must go back and warn the Elders about the Bloodfin.

Cal looked at Jake's face, grey with pain. She tried to sound confident. 'If they do come back I'll draw them away so you can escape.'

'Don't be daft,' said Jake. He hesitated, then gave her a smile. 'But thanks.' Whoever she was he didn't want to be separated from her down here. Besides, it was a bit of big talk about his ankle – he wasn't really sure that he could swim at all.

'Tell me more about – about the Bloodfin,' said Jake, shifting to relieve the numbness of his good leg as he watched for any sign of shadows in the water beyond.

'I don't know much,' Cal replied. 'They come from the edge of the Ice Crust, where the Golden Eye only opens in the warming.'

'Golden Eye?' Jake was puzzled. 'You mean the sun!'

'My father will be able to tell you,' said Cal, 'although I'll be in enough trouble, going up to the Overbreath, let alone bringing back a Creeper.'

'Creeper!' exclaimed Jake. 'Is that what you call us? And what are you, anyway?'

'We're all Delphines,' said Cal. 'My people are called Silvertails. There are lots of Silvertail pods near here.'

A wave of fatigue distracted Jake. He sighed. 'Look, just tell me . . . if I'm not dead, why aren't I drowning?'

'I don't understand,' said Cal, intrigued by his presence in her world. 'Somehow you're like us. I know that the fathers of our race were Creeper men.'

Jake thought of the mermaid tales Charley sometimes told on a winter's night. Everyone knew they were only stories. None of it was true. There again, nobody would believe what was happening to him either. 'But how *can* I be here, talking to you?' he said.

Cal frowned and fixed him with a meaningful eye. 'Unnatural things have been happening.'

'What sort of things?' said Jake.

'I've only heard rumours,' said Cal. 'No one speaks of it much. But they say rogue currents are fouling the tides, stirring up murkwater. There are forbidden places, where unpredictable moods flow. And sudden sea furies . . .'

'That's what broke my boat,' interrupted Jake. 'That's just how it was – a sea fury, sudden like you say.'

'Yes. My father believes the sea is troubled.'

'Why?'

'I don't know. But he told me once about Merrows, the guardians of the ocean. Merrows had the gift of harmony – they ordered the balanced flow of the currents and kept peace between the creatures who shared the ocean.'

'What happened to them?' asked Jake.

'They died out long ago . . .' Cal fell silent and twisted a lock of hair between her fingers.

Jake remembered a picture made of shells set into the wall of the Anchor Inn – of a woman with a fish's tail, sitting on a rock, combing her hair. Inside the curve of her arm was a tiny, far-away sailor diving into the sea. 'Singing to him, that's what she's doing,' Charley had told him once with a wink. 'And he would drown in her arms, he would.'

'Do you think now they've gone, these Merrows, that the sea is . . . sort of, out of sorts,' said Jake. 'Unbalanced?'

A sad coldness seemed to chill the water around them. After a pause Cal turned to him.

'I don't know what is stirring up the water,' she said, 'but there's something about you – I think you can breathe like a Delphine, like us. We take one breath for seven tides.'

'Is that what you were doing by my boat? Taking a breath?'

Cal nodded. Suddenly a crusty scallop shuffled in the sand beside them and she was shaken from her solemn thoughts. 'Come on, there's no time to talk. We need help.'

The pain in Jake's ankle was making him weaker now but he followed her to the cave mouth, scrambling, half dragging his leg, and crouched low.

A shoal of small, speckled fish played for a while in a tangle of thong weed. Crabs edged around the rocks. Jake wasn't sure what they were waiting for. He was mesmerised by the creatures that scuttled and flitted past. Cal gazed, unblinking, into the distance. After a short while she felt faint, familiar vibrations in the water. Her heart leapt.

'Wait here,' she gasped. 'I'll be back.' With a beat of her

tail she dashed out into the open water.

Jake was gripped with alarm.

'Don't leave me!' Pushing off the seabed with his good foot he struggled after her.

Cal didn't look back. Jake's whole leg burned with pain, making movement jerky and slow. He had to rely on his arms, pulling himself through the water. Then ahead a huge dark shape loomed towards them. Jake panicked. Bloodfin! He turned instinctively to the light and swam for his life, up and up, crying hot tears. When at last he paused to look below Cal had vanished. There was nothing in the water. He'd lost her.

Five

To Strapkelp

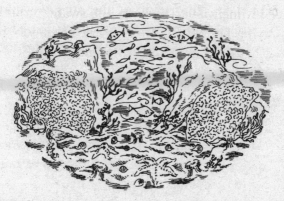

Jake kept swimming. Had a Bloodfin caught Cal? He wanted to go back, but instinct drew him to the surface. At last there it was, shimmering and shifting above. Jake stopped short, exhausted, treading water. He realised he had a choice. 'She said I've got breath for seven tides,' he told himself. He didn't have to go back up there, he could stay underwater. Jake's body ached to be safe in his boat. But there was no boat any more.

Thud!

Something heavy smashed into his side. Jake spun round. Wheeling beyond him was the undulating kite shape of a manta ray – a giant, bigger than his boat – and lying on its back, hitching a ride, was Cal. She held on to the rim of its wing, hair streaming behind as if she was flying. Jake laughed with relief. Bloodfin! What a bonehead!

The ray doubled back and came up slowly behind him.

'Where were you?' shouted Cal, beckoning him to catch the other wing. Jake stretched out, just managing to grab hold, and with a gentle heave the ray glided off through the water, quickly gathering speed.

Jake held tight. The ripple of the ray's powerful wing rolled him from side to side. It soared through the water, banked, then dived to skim low across the seabed before rising once more. It's showing off, he thought. Cal took one hand away and swung recklessly. Jake knew she was daring him to do the same, but he was gripping so hard his hands were numb. He couldn't let go.

A shoal of whiting darted out of their path and took shelter in the tentacles of a jellyfish. Jake spotted a big bass that turned away with a pout. Beneath them the seabed spread like a fantastic garden, blooming with starfish, sea fans and anemones. Everywhere crabs and fish skittered away from the ray's shadow. Jake had spent many hours staring down into the water from his boat but he'd never imagined anything as beautiful as this lay beneath the surface.

Before long his arm began to ache. Cal laid her face against the ray's head and stroked it with her cheek. The ray slowed. Cal pointed to an outcrop of rocks where shafts of bright water danced through silky seaweed. As they drew close she let go and slipped off the ray's wing. Jake was

Manta Ray

relieved to relax his grip. He stroked the ray's back gratefully and sank onto the sandbank next to Cal.

Cal looked around, listening keenly for any sight or sound of the Bloodfin. She had no idea about what they were doing but she'd tasted menace in the water around them. And they had mentioned others. How many? How close? The ray circled wide above them. He was some comfort, thought Cal, but a ray couldn't outswim a marlin, especially with them on his back.

Jake pushed a mound of sand beneath his foot to relieve the pressure on his throbbing ankle. 'How much further?' he asked.

Cal looked at the wound – it had swollen up like a puffer fish. She tried to hide her fears. 'We must eat – it will keep you strong.' Jake nodded. She pulled a tuft of red seaweed from the rocks and handed him a fistful. Then she rummaged among the anemones until she found some pale green finger-like tubes.

'Sea squirts.' She handed him one.

Jake looked at it. Lil had occasionally brought home something strange to go into the cooking pot but he'd never seen anything like this.

'Go on, try it.' Cal gave him a nudge. Reluctantly Jake took a bite. The texture was soft and rubbery, the taste slightly sweet. Not as good as squid, he thought to himself after the third one, but not bad either. The seaweed was salty and strong. Jake was surprised to find he liked it.

It was an odd sensation eating underwater. At first Jake thought he would choke, but when he tried not to think how it worked he found he could swallow naturally. Soon, with Cal's help, he was picking off kelp and sea squirts as if he'd been eating them all his life. He even prised open a green urchin, although after a lot of work there didn't seem much to eat inside. Cal showed him how to pluck a quill from a spiny fish and winkle out molluscs, and how to suck the fruity juice from plump, plant-like creatures she called bursters.

'What about this?' Jake spotted a round, orange sponge. He stretched out towards it but the sponge rocked away. A wave of pain shot up Jake's thigh.

He rolled in the sand, clutching his leg.

The surprised sea orange bobbed up to reveal a startled hermit crab beneath.

'Let me see,' said Cal. 'I don't think you'll make it all the way home like that.' She rubbed the fingertips of one hand over the webs of the other, back and forth, thoughtfully. It was too dangerous to leave him, wounded and weak. They had to get out of open water as soon as possible in case they met the Bloodfin.

'In Strapkelp forest, on the other side of this bank, there's a healer called Orcara,' Cal said. 'Maybe she has weeds to heal your leg. I can take you there but I can't stay. Whatever the Bloodfin are doing in our waters my father and the pod must know.'

Jake didn't like the sound of that. I'm completely dependent on her, he thought. I've got no idea where I am – how far from land, even how deep. I can't swim and my boat is wrecked. He was determined not to be separated from her.

'You don't have to leave me anywhere. I can make it,' he said.

'Says who!' retorted Cal.

For the first time Jake looked her straight in the eye. Eyes clear as gemstones. He knew she was right.

'Now watch!' Cal moved to a clearing and began to swim

30

in a circle, tipping her tail to create a rhythm in the water. Jake felt the powerful pulse but he was not the only one. In a moment the manta ray appeared, gliding towards them.

'You called it!' cried Jake.

'Him.' Cal was pleased that Jake was impressed. 'Skimmer. He's mine. Though he doesn't always come when he's called. Like me, I suppose!'

Jake lay once more on the ray's back and rested his cheek on its smooth skin, just as he'd seen Cal do. He felt the gentle creature's patient trust. 'I wish I understood anything at all about this place,' he sighed to himself, 'or even what is going to happen next.'

Skimmer took Jake and Cal, slowly this time, towards a low ridge that rose before them. Jake's mind drifted, as the pain became more intense. His eyes grew heavy. His body wanted to give in to the rocking motion of the ray's wing. Cal stretched across and held him. Skimmer reached the ridge. Without warning he nose-dived down the other side into deep water, as if soaring over a cliff edge and plummeting into empty sky. Jake came to with a start and dug his fingers into the ray's flesh. The water grew cold and dim as they descended. Jake strained to see any distance. Skimmer levelled out and slowed once more. Before them spread a dark forest of towering kelp: its thick, strappy fronds stretching a hundred feet high towards the distant light above. A multitude of fish slipped in and out of its forbidding depths.

'She's not going to take me in there,' Jake said to himself. He summoned all his remaining strength to resist. But Cal pulled him off Skimmer's wing and took his arm across her shoulder. Once more she looked him in the eye, sternly this time.

'You've got to trust me, Jake.' With a wounding flash she remembered her father saying almost the same words to her that morning.

Jake nodded weakly. Trust her, he thought. I've got no choice! He limped forward, and Cal led him into the forest.

Six

Orcara's Den

The giant kelp was dense and claustrophobic. It tangled itself around Jake's arms and legs and slapped him in the face. Dogfish and lumpsuckers hunted in and out of the roots and there was a constant noise of tiny whistles and clicking sounds.

Although Cal had passed Strapkelp before, she had never been allowed to venture inside and, inquisitive as she was, had never wanted to stray into its creepy maze. She had no idea how to find Orcara's den but she wasn't going to let Jake know that. She pushed forward, pulling him beside her, hoping that they would soon come across some sign of passage or habitation.

After what seemed like hours of struggling the kelp thinned out and tunnel-like passageways appeared. Cal stopped to let Jake rest against a root clump.

'We must be nearly there,' she said, picking up a shell that had caught her eye. 'When you meet Orcara, don't show her that you can speak or understand our language. Just pretend you're dumb.'

'Why?' Jake was feeling tired and irritated. 'Why can't I speak to her?'

Cal hesitated. 'She's not like us. Nobody knows much about her. She lives here alone, away from the pods.'

'But you said she was a healer?'

'I've heard she has those skills. We haven't got much time. Your wound is bad. It's strange enough that you are here at all. The fewer that know and the less they know the better.'

Jake was too exhausted to argue. 'I won't say anything. But what's a pod?'

'It's a kin-shoal,' said Cal, 'sometimes just a few Delphines living together, sometimes many. There are pods of Silvertail Delphines, then there are Bluestreaks, Duskins and others. They all have their own homewaters. You'll see.'

Cal pulled Jake to his feet once more and they continued along the path, which widened now and then as other paths crossed it. At last she stopped and listened. She heard a faint grumble, a guttural sound.

'We're here.'

At first Jake saw nothing but then he made out a solid wall of kelp in front of them, with a small parting for a low doorway. Cal shut her eyes and sang a long, plaintive note. Jake had never heard such a haunting sound before. It was Cal's calling sign. After a moment a tremulous moan rose and faded in answer. Cal smiled unconvincingly at Jake and,

before either of them had time to think about it, heaved him
through the doorway into the dark interior.

Orcara's den was a vast, cavernous structure like an
upturned basket of loosely woven, living kelp. Jake and Cal
stared wide-eyed. In some places the weed was knotted
together, in others twisted, or plaited and here and there
bunched untidily into thick sheaves. It reminded Jake of
some knitting he'd seen once, full of lumps and holes.

Small objects hung around the walls: tiny bottles suspended by twine looped around their necks, a bunch of
spoons, old keys of various sizes and short lengths of chain,
all lit by a phosphorescent glow coming from a mass of
algae hanging from the domed roof.

Jake stumbled. Cal, with her arm still around his shoulder, guided him to a heap of sealskins lying against the wall
of the kelp cave. Jake sat back thankfully. He was about to
ask where Orcara was when Cal twisted slightly and tipped
her tail. Jake understood at once she was gesturing towards
the far side of the chamber. He made out a huge mound of
knotted seaweed, this time heaped in a pile the size of a
beach hut. Looking closer he saw it was tangled up with
shells, twine, fragments of cork and crabs' claws, the sort of
flotsam and jetsam he loved to trawl through at the tide
line. But there was no sign of Orcara.

Then the whole mound heaved and shook, and a shower
of slugs dropped from its fronds. To Jake's horror a

withered finger emerged halfway up the heap. It grew into a gnarled hand that stretched up, parting the seaweed to reveal a small face, white as bone, with hooded yellow eyes and cruel lips.

Orcara!

Her mess of hair, with a matted skullcap of algae, had been extended with lengths of kelp and thong weed to the floor and threaded with small bones, beads of glass and sea trinkets. It was so long and thick that her body was completely hidden. Another hand reached out and grasped the staff leaning against the wall beside her. Jake had seen something like it in the harbour museum at home. He recognised the spiral twist along its length. It was a narwhal's tusk. A striped urchin shell had been pushed halfway down for a hand rest. The tip was worn smooth and he could just make out patterns carved around it. Leaning on the staff, Orcara rose and propelled herself, slowly, towards Cal.

For a moment, as they faced each other, the water around them tensed with apprehension. Jake noticed Cal's fist clenched tightly at her side. He wanted to leap up beside her but all he could do was watch in silence as he'd promised. Then, to his relief Cal opened her fist and handed Orcara a jade cowrie shell with an intricate lace pattern. Jake hadn't noticed her picking it up earlier. Orcara lifted the shell to the light and smiled, revealing a solitary tooth – sharp and serrated, like that of a shark. Now Cal spoke. Jake tried to hear her words but could make no sense of them. He lay back on the seal pelts, slipping in and out of consciousness.

Orcara moved towards him and bent over his ankle. The touch of her slimy hair against his leg roused Jake. He recoiled in horror.

She turned to Cal.

'I could heal him, but there'll be a price to pay.'

Cal hadn't thought of that. She swam to the entrance of the den.

'My father will reward you,' she said. 'I'll be back for him with the tide.' And with a deft flick of her tail she was gone.

Orcara smiled. This time her single tooth hung viciously over her lip.

'Your father won't reward me for this, my precious delphling,' she chuckled after her. 'Oh no! You'll pay for it yourself. If only you knew how much you will pay!' Then, seeming to summon supernatural strength, she raised the tusk staff above her head, mumbling and spitting as she lifted her face to the bright glow. With a sudden shriek she plunged the tusk down towards Jake's ankle. Jake tried to pull his leg away but he was paralysed with fear.

'NO!' he cried.

Seven

The Tide Turner

Cal began to search for a way out of the forest, relieved to have left Orcara's den. She marked her route by pulling down long fronds of kelp and tying one to another as she went.

Now I can find the place again quickly, she thought, and we can escape fast if we have to.

She felt guilty about leaving Jake in that foul place.

'But I had to do it. He couldn't make it any further,' she told herself. 'And she did agree to help.'

Cal had heard stories about Orcara – that Duskins travelled from their homewaters to seek her cures; that she could heal a broken fin by laying her hand upon it.

However, there were other tales – from urchin farmers who said she caused their crops to fail and storms to ravage the seabed; rumours that she could actually sour the currents and even transform herself into a seal to prey on unsuspecting pups. She was certainly known to practise charms and chants. Pelin had always dismissed these whispers with scorn. He said Orcara was simply a solitary creature of the kelp, lost in her own weird mysteries. But what would he say when he found out what Cal had done; not only ignored his warnings, but befriended a Creeper and taken him into Strapkelp, to Orcara herself? She shuddered to think of her father's rage. Yet Cal hadn't intended it all to happen. The sea had carried her to Jake and wrecked his boat – maybe wayward currents really were causing disruption. Had they brought the Bloodfin too?

The Bloodfin! Cal had an idea. If she could find them and discover why they'd come to Silvertail waters the pod would be grateful – then her father might forgive her for what she'd done. It was a dangerous plan. The Bloodfins' intentions were certainly not peaceful. But Skimmer would help her track them. She'd be safe with him . . .

Cal continued on through Strapkelp. Twice she doubled back on herself but at least the trail showed where she'd passed. When at last she emerged from the forest she spotted a broken lobster pot and dragged it over to mark her exit.

Then, without looking back she swam up to the ridge and signalled urgently for Skimmer. But Skimmer didn't appear.

'Where are you? I need you – it's important.' Cal repeated her call in every direction, but there was no sign of the ray. Annoyed, she set off alone.

Cal was a fast, agile swimmer, but how could she begin

to find the Bloodfin by herself? There was nothing for it but to return to the shallows and try to trace their scent.

As Cal streaked through the water she puzzled about everything that had happened since she left home. Who was this Creeper boy with the Delphine breath? There was no natural explanation for Jake's presence in the water. Since the moment she'd pulled him out of the storm into the cave some echo of a half-forgotten tale had been lurking in the back of Cal's mind. She had tried to dismiss it, too extraordinary to consider, but now it plagued her once more.

Many seasons before a pod of Drifters, nomadic Delphines, had stayed for a while at the sunken village, with the Silvertails. Pelin had reluctantly allowed Cal to befriend a young Drifter who had told Cal a secret. She'd overheard the Elders of her pod discussing a prophecy and talking of a stranger. A fearful time would come, they'd said, when the currents grew unruly and the Sea Spirit would be tormented by treachery. But one would come with the power to stem the dark flow. One who was of their kind but not of their kind. He would be called the Tide Turner.

'What does it mean?' Cal had asked.

'I don't know,' she replied, 'but they spoke in hushed voices and they were afraid. I dared not listen longer.'

Cal remembered asking her father about the prophecy later. He'd put down his tools and swept the hair away from her face, plaiting and tying it at the back, as he often did, so that he could look into her eyes. A tiny shrimp had scurried across Pelin's tail and he'd scooped it up in his hand. 'See this little shrimp?' he'd said, 'he'll scuttle around here, grow old and die in a handful of seasons. He doesn't worry himself with thoughts of destiny. Even the blue whale doesn't ponder on the sweep of the tides.' He let the shrimp scamper away. 'Don't fret about the future, Cal. Just learn to use your time well and be grateful for it.'

Then he'd grown solemn. Cal guessed he was thinking about her mother, Sylla. She asked no more.

But the story had haunted her.

Suddenly there was panic in the water. A shoal of mackerel flashed past. Hundreds of skipjack tuna raced frantically behind them and a seal dived across her path. Like all Delphines, Cal was sensitive to any variation of mood in the water. She smelt danger, she tasted change and felt minute vibrations across her skin. Instinctively she dived, down to the seabed where she hid among the broad leaves in a salt cabbage patch.

Moments later the cause of the panic appeared. A bolt of blue marlin streaked right over her head. Cal could make out their rapier-like spears and sickle-shaped tails and there, among them, two Bloodfin! The battalion of terrifying predators sped into the distance and was gone.

Without a second thought, Cal shot out of the cabbage patch and followed. This was her chance. It was the only way to find out what they were doing in Silvertail waters.

'If I stay in their slipstream I'll be safe,' she told herself, pushing the limits of her strength to keep them in sight. 'They must have just fed because they're only cruising. If they were hunting I'd never keep up.'

Cal swam streamlined now, arms at her side, using only her powerful tail to propel her through the water. But she knew she couldn't keep up that speed for long.

Luckily, just as she felt her body tiring, the big fish slowed, scattered and came to rest, weaving discontentedly above the seabed, prodding stones and shells with their spears. The two Bloodfin disappeared between some pillars of rock. Cal stopped a few yards off. The marlin didn't seem to notice her but she was taking no chances. She worked her way forward, gliding in a low, wide arc beyond them, and came to a cluster of thick chimney crags, ragged with weed. Sharp voices came from within.

Cautiously Cal peered between the crags. There they were – six young Bloodfin, not much older than herself, armed with knives, spears and harpoons.

Eight

Bloodfin

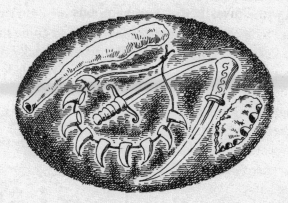

The Bloodfin were a fierce race known to be skilled hunters. They lived in the cold Melt at the fringe of the Ice Crust, where food was scarce and the sea itself froze hard as rock. They rarely ventured to warmer waters. Now she was closer Cal saw they were smaller than she'd imagined, compact, with wiry limbs. Their skin was marked with scar patterns, just the same as those she and Jake had seen outside the cave. Most shocking were their cruel faces. One wore a necklace of claws; Cal had heard stories of ferocious bears that swam in the meltwater and she guessed it was a hunting trophy.

The young Bloodfin were edgy, twisting restlessly in the

43

water; two of them smashing shellfish against the rocks and another aimlessly hacking at the chimneys with a metal spike. Cal kept still, trying not to give herself away by any disturbance of the water.

One patrolled the chimneys, as if expecting trouble. He tossed a stone towards the marlin. A big beast instantly shot forward and smacked it with its snout, sending it spinning close to Cal, who shrank further into the shadows. She couldn't stop herself from trembling but she didn't want to move away until she'd heard what they had come for.

'You know the Lin are restless,' growled a stocky Bloodfin working barnacles off a piece of pipe with a blade. 'They won't be bound to us much longer. They're fighting among themselves now. They'll soon be skewering each other with those spears if they don't see more action. There's too much idle muscle out there.'

Marlin

The Bloodfin with the spike scowl-ed. 'They'll see action, Bait, if you have the gut for it!' Bait lunged towards him with the pipe but the others pulled him back, snatching the weapon from his hand.

'Where are the rest, anyway? Why do we have to hang around here?'

The patroller gave up his watch and came over to join them.

'Reefer took them to scout about for that Creeper we're supposed to find.'

'The living dead one!' The gang sniggered.

'Creepers! What a life, crawling around up there. Have you ever seen 'em swim! Ha! I saw it once – big, ugly brute, flapping around like a demented octopus!'

Cal edged closer. Could they possibly be talking about Jake? Her heart thumped so loudly she was terrified it would give her away. There was a pause while the patroller lifted the necklace to his face and picked his teeth with a claw. Two of the gang at the back of the group shifted uneasily. Cal saw them exchange urgent looks. She recognised the two who had paused outside the cave where she and Jake had been hiding.

'Seems this Creeper could be useful,' shrugged the patroller. 'We've got to deliver him alive, still squirming!'

Out of the corner of her eye, Cal saw the two Bloodfin edge silently away.

Now the youngest member of the gang, not much more than a boy, spoke.

'I don't understand . . .' The left side of his face twitched nervously. 'Why do we have to kill the Silvertails?' All eyes fell upon him.

'We have to kill them,' the patroller growled. 'They are many and we are few. We must make them fear us, because only their fear makes *us* the strongest. The Wrath is rising. It has begun.' A noose of chill water tightened around the rock pillars. 'The time has come when those who were denied will triumph and the favoured ones shall perish. We will be the first to strike – and we will lead the rest!'

'But what happened to the Elders? They'd have found another way—' The young one stopped, hearing the weakness of his words.

The patroller swam closer. 'There is no other way,' he snarled. '*We're* running things now and we don't want any trouble from Silvertails, or sponge-hearted snivellers.'

There was a pulse of stunned silence among the gang, then one of them smirked.

'Hey, Sniveller, shark got your tongue?'

Suddenly the patroller froze.

'Where are Leaper and Barb?'

Cal started with alarm. She had to get away. Capture the Creeper! Kill the Silvertails! It was too terrible to be true. Cal fled, her body trembling uncontrollably. She had to reach the pod. She was the only one who could warn them. Spotting a shoal of mullet cruising fast above, she slid in among them to disguise her scent.

Cal swam on with the shoal, which kept a course just off the shallows. Her mind raced. All the Silvertails were in danger. And how could the Bloodfin know about Jake? Suddenly Cal heard voices ahead. So, she had been seen! Leaper and Barb had circled to head her off. She saw them first, knives glinting in their fists. Cal twisted round and shot away from the mullet. Ahead rose a low sandbar and beyond that she could see the rippling fronds of an eelgrass meadow. If only she could make it that far she might be able to lose them, but she was in shallow water now and the tide was slowing her down.

'Keep going,' she gasped, urging herself on.

The two Bloodfin weaved in and out of each other's path, testing their skills as they made a race of it. At last Cal reached the sandbar and dived into the thick eelgrass on the other side. She snaked into the heart of it, low to the ground. If the water had been deep her track through the fronds would have been easily visible from above, but the dense, narrow grass grew right up to the surface. Cal paused and tried to calm herself. She knew the taint of her fear in the water would lead the Bloodfin straight to her hiding place. She listened. There was no sound and yet – she could smell them, close – then, to her relief, turning away.

Suddenly there were other voices – two more Bloodfin had caught up with Leaper and Barb.

'There's a Silvertail, she's here somewhere.'

'So that's where you went? Leave it. We're moving off.'

'But she might have heard – she'll warn the others . . .'

'And what? Those finless farmers won't put up a fight. We'll hunt them out of their hiding places. More sport for us!'

Cal shuddered at the sound of their laughter as they leapt back over the sandbar four abreast.

She glided to the ridge of silver sand, waiting awhile to be sure the Bloodfin had truly gone, then slipped over and down the bank on to a dune. Their words had filled her with dread. It was true; her people had never had to defend themselves. Could they possibly be forced to leave their settlements, their homewaters? She thought of Nerine, the oldest and weakest in their pod, who could only reach the Overbreath now on the backs of others, and the young ones who had never swum in the open sea. Where would they go? She was exhausted but there was no time to rest.

'I have to go on,' she told herself, 'I have to get home.'

Cal swam nervously into open water and took her bearings from the taste and flow of the current. I must be upstream from Strapkelp, she thought, as there was no trace of its pungent scent. She swam deeper and found a cool, fast-moving channel, which she hoped was heading for the confluence that gathered beyond the forest. Cal felt alone and afraid. She scanned the water as she swam, hoping she might find company from seals or a turtle heading the same way. Why did I leave, why did I have to know more? she thought. If only I'd been content. Father loved me, why wasn't that enough? Cal reached for her pendant. Was it only her guilt that made her feel responsible in some way for the trouble she had found?

Cal was shaken from her thoughts by a familiar beat in the water ahead.

'Skimmer!'

The manta ray sliced through the blue water, wheeled behind Cal and scooped her up on his wing.

'Let's get out of here!' Cal clutched his furled horn and buried her face in his back as he lifted her away.

Chapter Nine

Warning

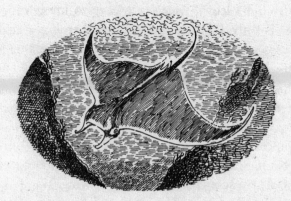

'Where have you been?' Cal kissed Skimmer's brow and stroked his sleek head gratefully. She didn't expect a response. Unlike other creatures, who communicated with sound or scent, Skimmer never gave any signals. But Cal knew he felt her touch and understood her voice because he reacted to her directions. Pelin said Skimmer lost his ability to communicate after Sylla died, almost as if the ray was mourning. He expected him to recover, yet he never did.

Skimmer had always roamed far and appeared unexpectedly and Cal had grown up looking forward to his visits. Over time they'd built an almost telepathic understanding of each other. Skimmer would sometimes accompany Cal and Pelin to the Overbreath, where he loved to thrill them with his acrobatics, leaping high out of the water and revolving in a slow, heart-stopping cartwheel before falling, with a flourish of his tail, back into the sea. Cal learnt to shoot out of the water and arch over his back, then to spin in the bubbles below until she was dizzy. As Cal grew older Skimmer took her on breathtaking rides; sometimes soaring like a switchback through canyons and sand chutes, sometimes drifting slowly; meandering above the seabed to search for shy fish and rare anemones. It was the only time Pelin allowed Cal beyond his sight.

She had never been so pleased to see him. Skimmer felt her relief as she lay on his back, her thumping heartbeat quickly calmed by the steady rise and fall of his wings.

'At least you arrived in time to save me from being captured . . . or worse.' Cal shivered at the thought of what might have happened if the Bloodfin had caught up with her. 'Take us home now, Skimmer, fast as you can.'

Cal was desperate to get back to the village and warn the pod about the Bloodfin, but now she also worried about Jake. If the gang were really searching for him would he be safe in Orcara's den? Surely the Bloodfin wouldn't hunt deep inside the kelp forest, but what if they found him?

The ray sensed her confusion. He increased his speed, making straight for the sunken village. Cal ground her teeth in desperation.

'Turn back, Skimmer,' she said at last. 'Back to Strapkelp. I can't leave Jake.'

Skimmer slowed briefly, but almost at once picked up the same course, gaining speed and swimming even faster.

'Strapkelp, Skimmer! Take me to the Creeper.' Still the ray wouldn't turn. Cal was shocked. He'd never been wilful like this before. She smacked her tail firmly against his back, but Skimmer wouldn't be persuaded to redirect his flight. Cal scowled.

'I can't go home yet, I can't go home!' And with a final slap of infuriation she let go of Skimmer's wing and set off for Orcara's den alone.

Ten

Dream

Orcara brought the tip of her staff down towards Jake's ankle with great force, but pulled back just short of his skin. For a moment she held it there, chanting, swaying in a trance. Jake was so terrified he seemed to disconnect from his body, as if the pain and fear were too much to bear. He found himself watching Orcara perform her mysterious rite as though he were floating around the den, circling the grotesque creature and looking down on himself, unable to move or cry out.

Orcara's muttering grew louder and louder then ceased abruptly. She cast the staff aside and raised her palms to the eerie light as if drawing it down into her hands. She seemed to draw Jake down again too. Once more he lay paralysed before her. She passed her bony hands across his leg and a rush of warmth flooded through his ankle. As his leg cooled the pain itself dissolved away. The wound healed.

Orcara touched Jake's eyelids with her withered fingertips and he slipped into a deep, calm sleep.

'Sleep well,' she hissed. 'You have two destinies to fulfil – yours and mine!' And mumbling to herself, she picked up the staff and shuffled into the depths of her lair. Behind, like a tail, slithered an eel with a V-shaped scar.

Jake opened his eyes in a dream. It was *the* dream; the one he'd had so many times before. He lay on a heap of tarpaulin in his boat, hands clasped behind his head, staring at a cloudless, blue sky. A warm breeze blew across his face and as it passed the sky rippled gently. Jake saw, as if for the first time, that it was not sky above him after all but clear blue water. A woman's face appeared through the ripples, a face with green willow eyes.

'Cal!' Jake called out. But even as he spoke he understood that it was not her. He knew those eyes, but this face was older with silvery hair. The figure dipped back beneath the water and Jake could see her swim, like an angel flying in a painting. He felt an overwhelming sensation of contentment.

Then, with the slightest splash, she emerged, carrying a small box, dripping with seaweed. She seemed to be offering it to him. Jake sat up in the boat and held out his arms. But instead of handing him the box the woman drew back, smiling. Jake stretched, reaching out . . .

'Wake up!' Cal had hold of his hands and was shaking them, pulling him from the bed in Orcara's den, pleading insistently in his ear.

'Wake up, we've got to get out of here!' She peered around the den. 'Where's Orcara?'

'Who?' muttered Jake, still half asleep.

Cal reached for a scrap of twine lying on the stony floor and hurriedly tied a knot message to warn Orcara about the Bloodfin. She fixed it to a furbelow stem by the doorway. She returned to Jake and roused him once more.

Jake groaned and pushed Cal away, angry at being woken from his dream. Then he looked round and remembered where he was.

'Sorry,' he said, sitting up.

'How's your leg?' she asked. 'What did she do to you?'

Jake looked and saw that his ankle was completely healed.

'I'm fine,' he said. 'I'm really fine.' He stood up. His leg felt strong. In fact, now he was awake, he felt invigorated, as if he'd plunged into the sea on a baking hot day.

'Come on, let's get out of here.'

Without another word they left Orcara's lair. This time Cal didn't use the trail that had brought her back through the forest so quickly. She was afraid that the Bloodfin might discover her markers. I hope Orcara finds my warning, she thought as she hurried Jake away in the opposite direction.

Cal couldn't read the water in the forest. There was no smell of open sea nearby because the salty tang of the kelp was overpowering, so she and Jake had to wander on blindly. They took it in turns to make decisions whenever they reached a fork.

'At least I can move faster,' said Jake. With his mind clear of pain he marvelled at the profusion of life in the bustling forest. Numerous shoals of fish flitted among the swaying fronds: whelks and urchins fed on algae-covered trunks and brittle stars hid among the holdfasts that anchored the kelp to the rock; young molluscs grazed the forest floor, which was thick with anemones, and ferocious fiddler crabs darted from crevices to hunt and fight.

Far above their heads the kelp glowed as light penetrated the fronds, but down below shadows danced. Jake was mesmerised.

However, Cal scanned the maze fearfully. A flank of scarred flesh stirred among the weed. She gasped and reached for Jake's arm. As the light shifted she saw it was only a patch of fretted shade.

'What's up?' asked Jake.

'Nothing,' Cal muttered. 'Let's go faster.' But in every dark blade she saw Bloodfin spears, in every thicket she glimpsed the brutal faces of Leaper and Barb.

They struggled on earnestly. As the glow above began to fade Jake realised it must be late in the afternoon. He'd lost all sense of time since the storm early that morning.

Cal noticed him push ahead with more determination.

She voiced his thoughts. 'We don't want to be caught in the forest at night.' Jake shook his head silently. It became harder and harder to find a way through the relentless wall of kelp. Jake wished there was a break, a glimpse of what lay beyond, something to measure their progress by.

'We could be lost in here forever,' he sighed.

'We mustn't get separated, whatever happens.' Jake heard the tense chord in Cal's voice. She looked drawn and tired.

'Look . . .' He picked up a sharp razor shell and cut a length of kelp from its stem, tied it around his waist and offered Cal the other end. She saw what he wanted her to do and looped it around herself, fixing it with a knot.

'That's better,' said Jake, pleased with himself. And on they went, fighting their way through the forest.

Eventually they came to a trampled patch of weed and Jake began to suspect they were going round in circles.

'Where are we heading?' he asked.

'Home,' Cal replied, pulling away at the puckered fronds that continually snagged her tail.

'But I thought you went home when you left me?'

'No. I went back to find the Bloodfin, to find out what they wanted.'

'That was stupid!' Jake stopped abruptly and the kelp tether snapped.

Cal swung away from him crossly and set about tying it together.

'No, it wasn't. I found out they've come to hunt down our people. I've got to warn my father.' Agitated, she fumbled with the knot, gave it a tug and began to move forward again.

'Cal, did they see you? What if you'd been caught?' Jake was astonished that she'd put herself in such danger.

'No one saw me,' Cal lied. 'I'll tell you everything when we get out of here.'

'*If* we get out of here,' he muttered.

A little way behind them Orcara's eel turned and hastened away to his mistress . . .

At last Cal and Jake found their way out of the forest and untied themselves.

'I'm not sure Skimmer will come if I call him,' said Cal, remembering how he had ignored her earlier. 'I'm not even sure that I should call him—' she scoured the open water '—we don't know who else might be listening out there.'

But as Cal pulled shreds of weed from her hair an unmistakeable silhouette glided towards them. With a graceful swoop Skimmer circled their heads, hovering impatiently. He seemed keen, like them, to leave Strapkelp at once. Within moments Cal and Jake were on his back and they set off at an alarming speed, up and over the ridge once more, then away into brighter waters past a stretch of rippled sands, sending startled flat fish shimmying away in their wake.

As Jake rocked across Skimmer's back he tried to focus on what had happened. It still seemed impossible that he should be there, underwater, and yet he had to believe it. He had to believe without understanding. Jake didn't doubt the danger in that place. What were those rogue currents Cal seemed to be afraid of? Who were the Bloodfin? He wanted to ask Cal so many questions but when he tried to speak the slipstream snatched his words. He gripped Skimmer's wing tight and scanned the water. Trouble could come from ahead or behind, above or below – anywhere in this water world.

At last Skimmer seemed to tire and slowed a little.

'We're almost there,' said Cal.

'First tell me what happened when you left me,' Jake insisted. 'I need to know. I can't – well, I'm just – oh, don't you see, it's impossible for me if I don't understand anything!'

Cal realised she would have to tell him everything that had happened at Chimney Crags, but she wasn't sure how to explain it when she couldn't make sense of it herself.

Jake listened in shocked silence as she described Bait and his gang and related what she'd overheard. 'But why? Why are they trying to find *me*?' He was horrified. 'I'm not one of you, I mean . . . I'm a boy! How do they know I'm here? And why do they need to kill anybody?' Skimmer banked and Jake was jolted hard against Cal. Their eyes met. He saw she was as frightened as him.

Cal turned away. 'Something truly awful is starting to happen. 'The Wrath is rising,' that's what they said.'

'What is the Wrath?' Jake felt warm sweat meet the cold water beneath his armpits.

'I don't know. When we've warned my father I'll take you back to—'

Skimmer stalled suddenly.

Cal fell silent. She stared ahead, her face ashen.

Eleven

Home

Jake couldn't believe his eyes. There before them was a ruined village. Stretched on either side of an invisible lane were tumbledown remains of a dozen stone cottages. Some were intact, although none had roofs, others were little more than fragments of wall with a chimneystack, or a windowsill. A little way beyond these was a broken well covered with barnacles, and near that a tall stone cross.

Fish swam in and out of open doorways and glass-less windows. The gardens were thick with seagrass and anemones. Strangest of all, the stones and bricks were free from barnacles and algae, unlike the crusted rocks of the seabed around them.

Jake gaped in amazement.

Cal slipped off Skimmer and began to swim frantically from one building to the next.

'Where are they?' she cried. 'Where have they gone?'

Cal turned towards her own home, set apart from the rest, at the end of the village.

'No . . .' she groaned. 'No!' With a swoop of her arms she raced towards the cottage. Skimmer and Jake followed. They caught her just as she reached the doorway. Cal stopped and sank to the sand.

'Father!' she screamed. The whole ocean seemed to shudder with her cry.

Jake scrambled off Skimmer and dropped to his knees beside her.

'We're too late! They were here! The Bloodfin were here! No, no, no.' She thumped her fists on the paving stones, then she began to beat them against her own tail. 'It's my fault. I could have warned them!' Jake took her hands and held them tight.

Skimmer twisted to and fro before the cottage in distress. Cal turned to him. 'Is that why you didn't come before? Were you here, trying to save Father? Why didn't I see? If only you could have told me—'

Shaking with tears Cal swam slowly inside and Jake followed.

The hallway was scattered with broken shell bowls and a pair of smashed clay amphora. A tangle of kelp and seal pelts was strewn on the stairs.

'Why didn't I come here first? I could have saved him . . . I could have saved them all!' She crumpled to the floor.

Jake wanted to say something, to do something, but he felt lost for words. He sat down close beside her. 'I'm sorry,' he said. 'I'm really sorry.'

Cal threw herself on to his shoulder. She cried desperately. Jake held her tight. 'It's my fault,' she said at last, rubbing her sore eyes. 'It's my fault. If I'd been here . . . if I'd listened to his warning, it's my fault.' She looked despairingly at Jake. His eyes answered with the words his voice couldn't find. Cal sank her head in her hands. Her copper hair hung like a shroud around her. Jake noticed the shimmer of silver running through it. He decided to leave her alone for a while.

Jake moved away through the house. He remembered how he'd been unable to wake Charley the morning the old man died. How he'd wanted to cry then, brimmed to burst with the feeling, but his eyes wouldn't make tears. It was only later that afternoon, when he'd made off on the boat that the tears had come. A whole sea of them. He wouldn't have wanted anyone then.

Jake looked around. In this strange world it was oddly normal to be in a house, even though it was a roofless ruin, and yet nothing could be weirder. Curtains of olive light rippled down the stairwell. A pair of weever fish burst out of the soft mud at his feet and scooted off.

In the nearest room many small objects lay on the flagstone floor and propped against the walls – a handbell, buckles, glass inkwell, even a barometer in a half-rotted frame, all arranged like precious possessions in a tiny museum. Jake guessed they must have been salvaged from wrecks. They were interspersed with heaped fragments of coloured shell, sea smooth glass and plaits of fishing twine. However, the other rooms were littered with broken things, mostly bottles and bowls. A twine curtain threaded with shells had been ripped from a doorway and in the back room he found an upturned lobster basket amid a mess of urchins and oyster shells.

Jake climbed the staircase, stepping carefully over the slippery pelts that seemed to have been flung there. In the first room above, a large piece of timber had been placed beneath a window. On it was a collection of metal implements: a trowel and scraping tool, some large twisted nails. More were scattered on the floor. In the next room an earthenware jug lay smashed beside an old iron bedstead. Immediately Jake's eye was drawn to a wooden box beneath it. His heart missed a beat. It looked just like the box in his dream. He crouched down and began to tug it from under the bed. Cal appeared at the doorway. 'Oh!' she exclaimed.

Jake jumped, embarrassed at being caught snooping. 'Sorry. I was just curious,' he said. But Cal wasn't looking at him. She picked up a handful of knotted twine from among the shards of broken jug. Had her father not even found the message she'd left for him?

'What's that box?' Jake interrupted her thoughts.

'It's mine,' said Cal, distractedly.

'Can I see it?'

Cal rubbed her eyes and threw the twine away. For a moment Jake thought she was going to cry again, but she swept the hair from her face and tugged out the box. Jake helped her heave it up onto the bed.

'It belonged to my mother,' said Cal. Her voice was small and shaky. 'I don't know what's inside. There isn't a key. My father didn't know either but he said she wanted me to have it.'

Cal remembered how she had pleaded with Pelin time and time again to break the small brass lock, but he had refused. She was pleased that Jake liked it.

Jake was fascinated. He stroked the dark wood. Although it was a plain thing there was something compelling about it. *How* could the box from his dream be here, in his hands?

They were startled by a crash downstairs. Without thinking Jake ran across the room. Cal darted forward to pull him back but it was too late. He reached the landing. She shrank back against the wall. But, to her relief, Jake turned with a grin.

'It's all right. It's only a pair of lobsters – big brutes fighting!' he said. 'They've knocked over that barometer.'

'I don't want to stay here any more,' said Cal. 'I want to be safe. I want to rest.'

'Let's take the box with us,' said Jake, hoping she wouldn't ask why. He had to get a look inside it.

Cal hesitated. She was so miserable and exhausted that she didn't want to think about it. Wearily, she lifted the box from Jake's arms and led him silently out of the house.

Jake followed Cal a short distance from the cottage to a small clearing in a crook of white dunes. Without another word she set the box in the sand, lay down with her tail curled around it and fell fast asleep.

Jake settled beside her. He desperately wanted to try opening the box but he didn't dare disturb her. He stared at the frown still creasing her forehead. Until that moment he'd been completely dependent on Cal in this underwater world; without her he'd be lost, hungry and probably soon dead. He'd relied on her knowing what to do. But suddenly, it seemed, things had changed. Cal was in trouble. She had no mother or father now. Her people were gone and even the sea was strange, so she said. She was strong all right, Jake could see that, but she'd been left so alone. No one was tougher than Lil, more able to take care of herself, but she'd always had Charley. She'd never lost everything, like Cal. He studied her domed forehead and her webbed hands clenched together under her cheek like a knuckle pillow. Cal was tough, but maybe she would need him for a while. She'd looked out for him after all.

Somehow, whatever bound him to Cal felt like a sort of belonging. It felt good.

Jake gazed out at the water, which was growing dark. All around him creatures of the daylight searched for the protection of caves and crevices while others, night feeders, emerged. Jake closed his eyes and listened to the chorus of squeaks and whistles that echoed across the seabed. 'I'll look out for her,' he said as he drifted off to sleep. 'And tomorrow I'll try opening that box.'

Twelve

Hope

When Cal woke she saw Skimmer resting nearby. He never slept deeply and at the first flicker of her eyelids he shifted close. The pale morning light played on the crystal water. A shoal of herring fry tacked past, like tiny slips of quicksilver. She sat up. There was Jake stretched beside her, arms crossed on his chest and a seahorse bobbing around his head. Cal trickled a pinch of sand on to his nose. He twitched and brushed it off in his sleep. The seahorse darted a safe distance away and, a moment later, returned to hunt for breakfast in Jake's thick curls.

Cal rubbed the sleep from her eyes and gazed down

towards the village. What a mournful, eerie place it was now. The only sound was the cry of a blue whale calf far away. She recalled how, just a few days before, she and Pelin had helped bring home a fine oyster harvest. As they'd pulled the nets into the village the whole pod had gathered to celebrate and prepare a feast. Then the Elders had chanted the old stories and there had been beautiful singing – such haunting songs that nightwater itself had hushed to listen. Now not one Silvertail heart beat among the ruins.

'What shall I do?' Cal felt empty and numb. 'I shall have to find a new pod, somewhere. There's nothing for me here.' But to leave her home was to leave her memories, all she'd ever known. She decided to swim down through the village one last time.

Cal made her way back, cautiously. At every turn she almost dared to hope she'd find her father, with open arms, alive and well. But then her memory replayed their last argument. She saw his face, older and sadder than ever. Since the day Cal's mother, Sylla, had died Pelin had taken care of their daughter himself, not accepting any help. Cal remembered him devoting all his time to her when she was very young, always patient to explain, always encouraging her confidence. She had loved their visits to the Overbreath. He used to laugh at her dancing in the big surf under the stars. 'Calypsia – my singing spinner' he called her.

Pelin had kept her away from the other Delphines. She had hardly noticed then because he was her whole world. But as she grew older Cal became curious about life beyond their home. She listened for hints of what lay outside the homewaters. She tasted traces of the unknown in the current and it excited her. That was when her childhood began to feel like a prison. She had started to resent her father's watchful eye and begged to be trusted. What *had* he been afraid of? She'd never understood. But she did know he'd only been trying to protect her. Why had she been so angry, so stubborn? She'd turned her back on him and now – now she'd give anything to bury her head on his shoulder.

Cal lay on the sand, wishing it would fold itself around her and smother her grief. He couldn't be gone. It wasn't true. 'If I'd been here we could have escaped together. We could have hidden, or fought them,' she cried. 'I'm selfish and stupid and . . . Father . . . where are you? Don't leave me alone!'

Cal wept hopeless salt tears into the great salt ocean. Drop by drop, the sea gently took her grief.

When at last she came to, Cal found Skimmer at her side. Something white lying in a clump of weed caught her attention. It glinted in the morning light. Cal reached out. It was a necklace, hung with white claws.

The Bloodfin! Skimmer started at her alarm.

'Skimmer, you must hurry to the Blue Caves,' said Cal. 'There's a large Silvertail pod there. Why didn't I think to warn them last night? They're the closest. It might be too late already!' Looking round, Cal saw a length of twine trailing from a nail. Snatching it up she began to tie a knot message. Cal was skilled with her fingers and, like all Delphines, knew hundreds of knots which could be tied in varied patterns or worked together in complicated plaits and braids. Hurriedly Cal made a warning for the Silvertails nearby.

'You'll be quicker without me, Skimmer,' she said as her fingers worked frantically, twisting and tying the twine. When it was done she put the message carefully between Skimmer's jaws and, laying her head against his, urged him to hurry. He nuzzled Cal's cheek, reluctant to leave her, but then with a graceful sweep of his great wings he took off and was gone.

It was some time before Jake began to stir. He felt the water around him and smiled. Despite the extraordinary events of the day before he was excited to wake up in this surprising adventure that had claimed him.

He looked round and couldn't see Cal. Then he remembered the box. It wasn't there either. Panic prickled through Jake's body. Had she taken it and left him?

He scrambled to his feet and swam off towards the village. The whole quiet sea felt abandoned. Surely Cal wouldn't have deserted him? And the box – he'd been certain it was important. He had to find them both.

'Cal!' Jake called as he neared the village. There was no answer. The gaping doorways and blind windows of the empty houses shrieked silently like faces stricken with horror. Jake shivered.

Suddenly he was startled by the harsh scrape of metal on stone.

Cal appeared, carrying a net basket bulging with tools, dishes and a shiny goblet.

'Why didn't you wake me? What's all that?' asked Jake.

'I've been thinking about what happened,' said Cal as she struggled to keep everything in her arms. 'I can't believe the Bloodfin arrived without any warning – there would have been threat in the water, creatures fleeing in fear. The pod must have sensed danger. Maybe some had time to escape.'

Jake remembered the vicious looking marlin he'd seen at the cave. He didn't rate anyone's chance of escaping from that. But he kept his doubts to himself. 'Where would they have gone?' he asked. 'Surely you don't need to bring all that stuff if you're going to search for them?'

'First I'm going to find Tarian,' said Cal. 'My father says nobody knows more about what's happening in the sea. If anyone escaped he might have news. But he doesn't give anything away.'

'Who is Tarian?' asked Jake as he took some of the dishes from her arms.

'He's a trader,' said Cal. 'He travels through the homewaters and Deep Sea, collecting and exchanging salvage from wrecked boats: tools, twine, sometimes food, and especially Creeper things – Delphines love to have Creeper things.'

Jake remembered the bell, the buckle and barometer in Cal's home. Then he recalled Charley's clutter of cuttlefish bones, shark's teeth and curious shells. Maybe they weren't so different . . .

'And a trader brings news from other settlements,' said Cal. 'Whenever he arrives everyone is eager to hear about what he's seen. Then, when the bartering is over, the Elders talk with him long into the night. My father always kept me away from them. He said a wanderer had no loyalty and couldn't be trusted.' She hesitated. 'But he did bring Tarian to our home once because he had a chain of keys and Father hoped he might be able to open my mother's box. None of the keys fitted. Then Tarian offered Father many things for the box, but he wouldn't part with it.' Her voice faltered. 'You don't have to come with me,' she said, not looking him in the eye. 'I'll take you up to the Overbreath, back to where you come from.'

Jake knew he couldn't go back yet. He couldn't just leave her, with her people dead and murderous Bloodfin out there – even if they really were hunting for him too. He made up his mind to help her somehow. Also, he had to get a look inside the box. He noticed now that Cal didn't have it with her. Had she left it somewhere while she collected those things? Before he could speak Cal asked him the very same question.

'Where did you put my mother's box? I have to take it with me.'

'I didn't move it!' exclaimed Jake. 'It was right beside you last night.'

Cal beat her tail in frustration. 'It wasn't there when I woke up,' she said, starting to get upset. She dropped a candlestick and then the basket tumbled out of her arms. Everything crashed to the ground.

The box had disappeared! Jake had been determined to open it somehow. He helped Cal put the things back into the basket and she took it from him.

'*Will* you come with me?' she asked quietly, with a shy glance.

Jake looked at Cal with her weighty basket and her tiny scrap of hope, all alone in a sea of danger. She needed him. Yes, he would help her. And he would find that box. He suddenly felt close to things he had to know, answers to questions he couldn't even put into words. Now he had seen the box from his dream, touched it, he was sure something of the dream itself must be real too. The uncertainty he had always felt about himself, the way the sea had taken him; there had to be an explanation and Jake was convinced the box was the link.

'I'll come with you,' he said.

Cal was pleased. She shook the hair from her face and the light danced on her freckled cheeks.

'So let me take the basket,' he said.

'No,' said Cal, 'I don't need any help.'

Jake shrugged and smiled to himself.

Thirteen

Tangler

Orcara had mended Jake's leg well and with his new strength swimming underwater was easy. He was relieved to leave the village behind.

Jake let Cal go ahead. But after a while he caught up and offered to carry the basket again. This time she agreed. She too seemed happier away from the village, having secretly convinced herself that her father was still alive somewhere. She handed him the heavy load and he strung it across his shoulders.

'Let's head for that reef, just beyond the sea fans,' she said. 'I think we'll find food there.'

Jake nodded. He was hungry.

Cal reached them first as Jake stopped to watch a bloom of milky white jellyfish rise towards the surface. As she had guessed, the reef was thick with good things to eat.

'All right,' Jake conceded. 'You're faster, but I'll still carry the basket.'

Cal handed him a piece of green algae.

'You're not so bad, Creeper,' she said, tearing another handful from the rock. 'But we mustn't stay long. It's too open here.'

'Where do you think the Bloodfin are now?' asked Jake, stretching for some seaweed he recognised from the day before.

'Well—' Cal looked into the distance, 'if they were heading for the nearest Silvertail settlement they'd have to cross Brightwater to the Blue Caves. I sent Skimmer there to warn the pod. I hope he arrived in time. But there are other Silvertails on the margin of the Upwelling and a big pod that live in a wreck near the Twister.'

'What's the Twister?' asked Jake.

'It's a deep channel in the rock where the current's forced at great speed.'

'It sounds a dangerous place to live,' said Jake, trying to satisfy his hunger as quickly as possible.

'It is perilous,' said Cal, 'but the pod know its moods. They live near the Twister because there's always plenty of food where the water's stirred up. And strangers don't go near.'

'So are all the Delphines called Silvertails?' Jake was still confused.

'No,' Cal said patiently. 'There are many different Delphines, all with their own homewaters; Duskins live at the rim of Deep Sea, Pearlflukes farm the Crystal Drift, where the sparkling water's warm. I'd love to go there. Further along the shallows there are Bluestreaks and in the downcurrent, of course, the Bloodfin, they hunt in the Melt at the Ice Crust.' Jake wished he had a map of the sea – a Delphine map. He decided to ask Cal to draw one in the sand later when they were in a safer place. Now he thrust a handful of algae into his pocket and helped her gather the bartering things together. His mind turned again to the box.

'Do you think Bloodfin came back and took the box?' he said. 'Surely nobody could get by Skimmer?'

'They wouldn't have stolen the box and left us sleeping,' said Cal. 'They'd have killed me and taken you. No, they must have moved on to search for another settlement. As for Skimmer, he often wanders away. It's the busiest feeding time in the open ocean. There's a great plankton feast, especially at this time of year. Small fish swim up for the plankton, the bigger fish swim up for the small fish – Skimmer loves to graze at night.'

'Then who could have taken it?' said Jake. He didn't like the idea of someone, or something, searching around while they were asleep.

'Why are you so interested?' asked Cal. 'It's *my* box.'

Jake felt embarrassed. He didn't want to tell Cal about his dreams.

'I don't know,' he lied. 'I like a puzzle. I bet I could open it for you.' He looked up and caught Cal's pained expression, as if something hurt and she didn't want to admit it. She started to swim away.

'I want to open it too. It belonged to my mother,' she mumbled over her shoulder and her words were carried away in a stream of bubbles. 'I want it too.'

Tarian's place was a morning's journey from Cal's village, further out to sea across the Ribditch – a rough, furrowed plain studded with spiny urchins and starfish. The water there was murky and Jake swam closer to Cal. He decided to approach the subject of the box again by asking about her mother.

'I was only small when she died,' Cal said. 'I don't remember her.'

'Didn't your father tell you about her?'

'It made him sad to speak about it, so I never asked.'

At once Jake felt the water around Cal cool, as if her body warmth had dropped. It cast a chill upon him too.

'I'd like to know about my mother, my real mother,' he heard himself saying. The thought surprised him.

'What do you mean?' Cal realised she hadn't considered whether Jake had any family.

'Well, I was found in a boat when I was a baby. That one you saw me fishing in. It was pulled up on the beach. No one knew who left me there.'

Cal was shocked. 'Who took care of you?'

'I did have a dad,' said Jake, smiling as he saw Charley's face in his mind. 'A good dad. And a mother too. But there must have been – you know, the one that left me in that boat. I think my real dad must have been a fisherman because—' Jake suddenly felt he'd said too much. 'Anyway they've gone now, all of them.' His brow knotted. 'And the boat's gone too.'

'So you're alone, like me?' she said.

Jake nodded and turned away. He heaved the net bag higher up his back. He'd had enough talk.

They swam along in silence for a while. The water became dull greyish green, clouded with floating debris from the siltbed below. Then Jake saw a stack of rusty metal ahead. It looked like a buckled section of ship's hull. When they drew closer they found an enormous anchor propped against a rock and more jagged metal plates, some half buried in the sand.

'Is it a shipwreck?' asked Jake.

'No. It must be Tarian's place. We're nearly there,' said Cal, leading him through the wreckage. As they went on the heaps appeared more deliberately arranged, like the organised chaos of a scrapyard. Great broken pieces of hull were filled with jumbled chains, propellers and curious bits of ship's fittings that Jake couldn't identify.

They swam further, now weaving a passage between junk that towered several feet high. Every shadow taunted them with the silhouettes of fins, spears and marlin spikes. Jake scanned the dark spaces nervously. Cal strained every sense to read the water around them. Lobsters scuttled over the wreckage and crabs scrambled in and out of crevices. The whole place echoed with the deep groan of metal shifting in the current. It sounded to Jake as if the earth itself was in pain. He imagined the screams of drowned sailors and the tangle of their trapped, ghostly limbs . . .

Cal swam nearer to Jake, so close that her hair strayed across his face. 'Look! That must be where he lives.' She pointed between two mountainous heaps of rope. Jake stopped in his tracks.

'An old submarine!' But he didn't get a chance for a closer look.

Thwack! A muscular tentacle whipped around his body and thrust him to the sandbed. In the blink of an eye Cal thudded down beside him and a giant octopus lowered its body on top of them both. Jake fought fiercely, pulling the tentacle away from his chest only to have his arm pinned down by another.

Octopus

'Cal – can you hear me?' he puffed, pushing vainly at the heavy, grey flesh settling on his legs.

Cal spat out curses as she wrestled with the octopus's writhing limbs. She'd forgotten about Tangler, Tarian's scout! He smacked her hard with a sucker.

Suddenly, as Jake flung his arm out, his hand hit the bag lying just above his head. He closed his fist around the base of a goblet and tugged, but it was trapped in the net. With a desperate yank he loosened the goblet and pulled it free. He crashed it down on the octopus's body. Tangler reeled, but almost instantly recovered, his weight rolling painfully across Jake's legs. A tentacle wrapped around Jake's wrist and shook the goblet from his hand. Jake felt a pause – Tangler had seen the bag. The rubbery suckers eased their grip. Tangler released his captives, slithered off their bodies over to the bag and picked it up.

He squirmed, wriggling his great arms in delight.

'Those aren't for you,' Jake shouted furiously, rubbing his sore legs. He kicked the octopus hard, but Tangler wouldn't be distracted from the bag. Drawing it close to his body he sidled off through the wreckage towards the submarine.

Jake turned to Cal. She lay, motionless, on the seabed.

'No!!' He scrambled over and lifted her head onto his

knees, brushing the hair off her white face. 'What's the matter? Cal, Cal, open your eyes!' Jake shook her by the shoulders, pulling her up to rest against his chest. 'Come on, come on!' He shook her again, frantically.

Something slid alongside Cal's tail. The eel kept his scarred cheek close to her body.

'Get out of here!' Jake lashed out with his fist, letting Cal slip from his arms. But, to Jake's amazement, as she fell to the sandbed she came to. Cal raised her head, dazed and blinking.

'What . . . what happened?'

Jake helped her up. He almost hugged her.

'You were knocked out – there was an octopus. Remember? I thought it was the – never mind. You're all right, now.'

Cal screwed up her face and rubbed her head. 'It must have been Tangler – he's – he's Tarian's scout. I'm sorry . . . I should have remembered.'

'We were lucky he didn't crush us to death,' said Jake, '. . . or strangle us. Don't know which is worse. But he took your bag and headed off towards the sub.'

Cal sighed. 'Let him have it.'

'What about Tarian? You wanted news . . .'

Cal buried her head in her hands. 'There won't be any news,' she said quietly. 'My father's dead. I know. I know it's true. It was only a hope.'

Jake couldn't bear to see Cal defeated. 'Look, I'm going to get that bag back,' he said. 'We might as well try. You'd hate yourself for not trying.'

Cal looked up and smiled weakly at Jake. He was right. She would hate herself for not trying. How did he know that?

Her smile was all the encouragement Jake needed.

'Stay there. I'll be back.' And he made his way, warily, towards the submarine.

Jake was taking no chances. He kept his back to the walls of wreckage. In front of the submarine was a sandy clearing strewn with chains and piles of fishing net and a jumble of plastic containers strung together with nylon rope.

As he peeped between the salvage Jake saw the octopus appear from the hatch and slither down the side of the submarine, still nestling Cal's bag close to his body. Keeping to the shadows, Tangler scrambled alongside the sub towards a cliff on the opposite side of the clearing. He stopped beneath a crack in the rock. As Jake watched, Tangler unrolled a tentacle and pushed the bag into the hole. That's his hiding place, thought Jake with delight. Then Tangler tugged some weed from the cliff face and stuffed it into the crack.

Jake made a dash for safe cover behind a broken stone column. He had no idea how far an octopus could see, but he guessed it might sense his presence. Tangler returned to the sub and slumped down before it like a guard dog, idly twitching the tip of a tentacle.

'Come on, rubber-legs,' Jake muttered. 'Haven't you got somewhere else to go?' He guessed Tarian was not at home, and that Tangler's exploits were his own secret business. Jake picked up a small rock and threw it down one of the avenues of junk. It landed with a clatter. Tangler hurried off to investigate. Now Jake sped across the clearing and swam up to the crack in the rock. Dragging out the weed he reached inside and felt the bag. As he pulled it out his hand knocked against something smooth and hard. The box! So, Tangler had stolen that too! Jake was alarmed to think of the octopus groping around Cal and Him as they slept. Ugh!

Hurriedly, Jake dragged the bag from Tangler's hiding place and put it on the sand. Then, pulling out the box he set that beside it. A piece of tarpaulin lay nearby. He grabbed it and spread it out, placed the bag and the box in the middle, tied the corners together and heaved the bundle over his shoulder. Then he raced back to Cal, half leaping, half swimming, his heart beating so loudly he thought it would give him away.

'I've got the bag and, guess what – the box!' Jake grinned. He looked expectantly at Cal, hoping she was impressed. Her green eyes sparkled beneath her long lashes. 'Thank you,' she said.

'I don't think Tarian is here,' said Jake. 'He must be travelling. Let's get away quickly before Tangler finds us again.'

Now Cal took the bag and Jake wrapped the box once more in the tarpaulin and they made their way out of Tarian's place through the alleyways of wreckage.

When they came to open water they stopped for Jake to rest. Cal unwrapped the box and laid her webbed hands upon the lid.

'Let me try to open it,' Jake said.

'I've tried hundreds of times,' she sighed. 'And Father and I searched everywhere for a key.'

'Let me try.' Cal hesitated, then drew back to let Jake kneel close. Slowly he took hold of the lid and lifted it. With ease it opened wide.

Fourteen

The Box

Cal stared over Jake's shoulder into the box.
'How did it open like that?' she gasped. 'How did you do it?'
Inside was a bundle wrapped in ragged, blue sailcloth.
Jake hesitated. 'It's your box,' he said. 'You look.'
'No,' answered Cal quietly. 'It never opened for me.'
They glanced at each other. Cal suddenly felt shy of this Creeper boy. Somehow the box must have been waiting for him. As she'd guessed, their lives had not mingled by chance – they'd been drawn together by the power of the fatestream. But why? Who *was* he?
Jake was nervous; he'd been so sure there was something

for him in the box he was afraid now of being disappointed. Tentatively he drew back the cloth.

Beneath it was a shimmering bubble of air filling the whole body of the box – and inside that was another, smaller bundle, this one bound with silver cloth.

Cal touched the bubble gently with her fingertip. It rippled and billowed, but didn't burst.

'I think we need to break it in the air,' said Jake, thoughtfully, 'in the Overbreath. Looks like whatever is in it has been put there to keep dry. We might damage it underwater.'

'It's a long way up from here,' said Cal. 'Maybe we can catch a ride.' Once more she swam in a circle as she'd done before to call Skimmer.

'Hey, what about Tangler?' said Jake, not taking his eyes off the box. 'We don't want to be ambushed again.'

'He won't come after us,' said Cal, 'he thinks he's guarding his treasure!'

To Cal's delight her call was answered by a huge sunfish. It was a curious, moon-shaped creature, about nine feet long, with almost no tail at all. It paddled slowly towards them, humming a low call sign. Cal replied with a swoop and dip of sound that reminded Jake of the flight of a bird. The sunfish swam up to her and Cal stroked its head. Then, seeing the box, it slipped away from her hands and came to nose about. Jake smiled and nudged the gentle creature with his shoulder. As it got more inquisitive and started to prod the bubble, he shut the lid and pushed it away.

Cal gestured towards the surface. The sunfish circled just above their heads, started to rise and then paused.

'It's waiting for us,' said Cal. Jake wrapped the box in the tarpaulin, knotting it this time into a rough sling which Cal hung over her shoulder. She led Jake to the sunfish. 'Take hold of her fin.'

Jake reached out. To his surprise the huge fish's body was covered with slimy mucus, but once they had a grip the sunfish began to swim upwards.

Sunfish

When they neared the surface Jake found the dappled sunlight on the water almost blinding. The sunfish gently tipped them off and paddled away to find herself a quiet spot to bask.

Cal broke through to the Over-breath first. She spat the water from her mouth and took a long breath of the invigorating air. Then she shook her head, spraying millions of diamond droplets into the blue sky, shut her eyes and raised her face to the warm sun.

But Jake hesitated, rocking in the rhythm of the water below. When Cal realised he hadn't followed she flipped upside down and dived back beside him.

'Come on,' she said, sensing his anxiety. 'We'll be safe here for a while. Look, so many creatures in the water – there are no Bloodfin here.' Sure enough the sunfish lay drifting on her side, unperturbed by a pair of gulls resting on the water nearby and a small shoal of Pollack idling along below.

'It's not that,' muttered Jake, 'it's just, it's sort of – going back.'

'You need a breath,' said Cal softly. 'It feels good, I promise. And we can look inside the box up there.'

Jake shook away his apprehension and with a sharp kick

of his legs made for the light. As he breached the surface he flung his arms above his head. A rush of oxygen shot through his body. He bobbed light-headed in the water, gasping and blinking; hanging between two worlds.

The warm, salty air smelt good. The gulls squawked loudly and he screeched back.

For a while Jake and Cal said nothing, simply enjoying the sunlight and the wonderful feeling of fresh breath in their lungs.

Jake studied the horizon. He made out a narrow ribbon of land where white cliffs rose from a rocky coast, notched with tiny inlets and coves. 'It's a long swim to the shore from here,' he said, 'especially with that box.' But Cal pointed in the opposite direction. Not more than ten yards away was a raft of matted seaweed and driftwood.

'There's a kelp paddy,' she said. 'Perfect.'

Far out at sea some large pieces of timber had become tangled up with lengths of rope and netting, all lashed together with tons of rotting kelp, ripped from its roots in a storm. Now the whole floating mass had drifted into the shallows, sheltering crowds of small fish in its trailing undercarriage. Despite the smell of decay and the haze of buzzing flies Jake and Cal heaved themselves onto the paddy. Luckily it took their weight, rocking and creaking with the swell.

Jake opened the box. Together they pulled away the sailcloth and Jake burst the bubble with his finger. Carefully

84

Cal lifted out the small, silver bundle. It glinted in the sun.

'What's inside?' Jake's stomach knotted in anticipation. He had no idea what to expect, but it must be something valuable, wrapped so finely.

Cal teased the folds of cloth apart and the silky fabric slipped through her fingers, so fine and fluid that it rippled across her hand like a tiny waterfall.

'But what's inside?' cried Jake.

'Nothing!' said Cal in dismay.

Nothing! Jake's heart sank. Nothing. He felt a fool.

But Cal was transfixed. She ran the cloth through her hands, feeling its deftly worked texture. Then she gripped Jake's arm. 'I was wrong,' she murmured. 'I think this is a message – it is – a message from my mother! Look – I've never seen knots so tiny. Oh Jake, these threads, they're lengths of hair!'

Now Jake stroked the astonishing message with excitement. How could anyone tie knots like these? He looked closely and saw the intricate design of plaits and braids woven together. 'What does it say?' he whispered.

Cal turned the message to find the beginning. Then she took the corner in her fingers, shut her eyes and began to read.

'*This is a message for the one who opened the box,*' she said slowly.

'That's me.' Jake's heart leapt.

Cal continued, '*And for the one who kept it. Sylla, your*

mother speaks to you across the tides of time.'

Her voice quavered.

'Go on,' urged Jake. What does she say?' He felt jealous that he could not read the message himself. Cal read on . . .

Fifteen

Sylla

'Calypsia, you lie asleep beside me. Too young to understand why I must leave you before morning. Too young to assume your birthright – a gift so precious that I must use my last strength to find it safe keeping.

I have much to tell you but little time.

Your grandmother, Til, kept a secret, which I did not learn until her lifeflow ebbed. Til was never strong. Her first born, Aran, could not tolerate weakness and had left us long ago, so I cared for her alone. When Til asked for one last breath I took her up to a sandbar near the shore. There she drew me close.

"Sylla," she murmured, "I am the last of the living Merrows."'

'What are the Merrows?' interrupted Jake.

'Remember,' said Cal, 'I told you about the stories? They were the guardians of the sea.'

'But I thought—'

Cal turned back to the message.

'"Although Aran lies long in the water, you are the first born of my nature," Til whispered. "Come closer. Use this gift – use it as the Spirit bids you."

And she breathed into my mouth – not the breath of days, but a force more vital. At once I felt woken from some half-life into brightness. I knew this was a Merrow breath, the gift of the Sea Spirit herself.

It was also Til's last. But Merrows do not die as others do. They return to the Sea Spirit. Remember this, daughter – we are with you.'

Cal paused. Jake could feel her tremble beside him as she rubbed her eyes. 'Go on,' he urged, 'don't stop.'

'After Til died I searched for Aran, unsure if I should know this sister who had abandoned us long ago. At last I found her. But Aran had changed. Her skin and hair were dark with dye, her mood dark with distrust.

She was unmoved by Til's death. Angry to hear of her gift. "The Merrow breath should pass to the first born!" she raged. "I was a strangeblood to her but I shall claim my inheritance. Be warned. I will take it – from you, or any daughter unfortunate enough to call you kin."

I fled from her.

For many tides I wandered aimlessly through the ocean. But at last the fatestream brought me to the shore. There I lay, lost and weak.

A Creeper was mending his nets nearby. He carried me back to the sea. But with each tide the waves returned me. The Creeper healed me and taught me to understand his tongue. As I listened to his stories I grew to love him. In turn I trusted him with my secret.

So I stayed there, caught between two worlds – unable to leave the water, but unable to deny my heart.

Then the Sea Spirit grew jealous, afraid that I might forsake the ocean. One night she cast a ferocious storm into the Overbreath. Lightning struck the Creeper's hut. Red fury consumed it. I tried to reach him, pulling myself over the sharp shingle, but the angry sea dragged me back. I could only watch from the crashing surf, wishing for legs to carry me across the stones.

No one came out through the door.

Once more I drifted through the ocean. But this time not alone. I began to feel the Creeper's child within me.

When it was time I found an empty shore. There our son was born. The child breathed easily under the water, but he had his father's form. Although he lay in the waves' cradle I saw he was stirred by windsong. I nursed him at the water's edge until I knew what I must do; I left him in his father's boat, at a place where he was certain to be found. Then I used Merrow skill to enable us to be together again one day, to give him the nature to inhabit our world. And I bound him to stay ever close to the voice of the sea.

'It is you, son . . .' Cal hesitated, stumbling over the words, 'it is you, my son, who revealed this message to your sister.'

Sixteen

Kin

Cal fell silent. Jake's heart thumped. Thoughts skidded madly around his head. This is what the dream had meant. It wasn't Cal, it was Sylla – his mother, calling him to the sea. Of course, the silver hair . . . this hair . . . He stroked the message. Overwhelmed, he tumbled off the paddy and plunged under the water.

'Jake—' Cal looked down. He swam furiously around the platform, diving and somersaulting, trying to obliterate a rush of confusing emotion. At last he came up with a tremendous splash.

'That's me!' He spun around, shouting aloud. 'That's me!'

'You – you're my kin,' said Cal, quietly. 'You're my brother.'

Jake stopped abruptly. He trod water, gasping for breath, his hair dripping around his startled face.

Cal stared at him, apprehensively.

'Did you know?' he asked. 'Did you know about me – about us . . . ?'

'No.' As soon as Cal said it she doubted herself. *Could* she have known, somehow? 'We were meant to find each other,' she said, 'I see that now. But I didn't know about Sylla – about us.'

Jake heaved himself back onto the paddy and lay down in the sun. He breathed deeply. For a while they both gazed in silence, searching for new bearings.

'It is . . . good, isn't it, being kin?' Jake said hesitantly, not looking at Cal.

'Yes,' she replied. 'It is good.' Jake rolled over and propped himself on his elbow. Cal's face relaxed and she smiled at him. 'When I left my father I didn't know what to expect. This makes sense of things – why I had to watch you, and the storm, don't you see, it was the sea claiming you back.' She twisted a strand of hair thoughtfully. 'But I haven't inherited this power my mother talks about. I mean, our mother.'

Our mother. Jake repeated the words silently in his head. *My mother.* Jake realised that apart from his boat nothing had ever really belonged to him: his home, Charley and Lil – all that suddenly seemed like something borrowed; some wonderful borrowed thing that he could never keep. Instead here was real belonging. And it felt like a new beginning.

'You haven't finished reading,' said Jake. 'Go on . . .' Cal turned again to the message.

'Three times that night I pulled myself to the water's edge, wanting to take you back. But the low tide kept me beyond reach. Early next morning an old Creeper found you and took you away.

I couldn't leave that place. At last a powerful undertow dragged me below. The current carried me until a ray appeared and took me to a Silvertail settlement, to others of my kind.'

'Skimmer!' cried Cal. 'It was him – he must have found her.'

'I hid my Merrow secret. Yet, in time, Til's gift moved me. Slowly I grew close to one who was kind. Pelin was overjoyed when you, Calypsia, were born and I saw Til's nature in your eyes. But that effort was great. Now I fear—'

Just then there was a riotous screech and three big gulls tumbled out of the sky, squabbling as they dived for fish beside the paddy. Seeing the silver cloth, one of them broke away and began stabbing at it with its beak.

'Get off!' Jake swung his fist. But the fearless gull thrust out its yellow claws and beat its wings at Jake's face. The other birds joined the attack.

Cal cowered. They shrieked and snatched at her hair. 'Jake, help me! Get them off!' She was frightened of the birds, afraid of tearing the message by pulling it away.

'WHOOA!' Jake shouted and leapt up. The paddy rocked. Suddenly there was a loud crack and a rotten timber that had been supporting the structure split in two. The gulls screamed and took off at once. The whole raft of weed collapsed beneath Jake and Cal, dragging them under the water in a convulsion of wrack and rope. They thrashed and twisted, struggling wildly to free themselves. Trapped air bubbled to the surface. Frantic fish scattered in panic. Jake could see nothing in the swirling debris. He pushed at the mat of kelp above his head, forgetting his Delphine breath, terrified that he was going to drown. Cal's hair was caught in a knot of cable. It pulled her down, headfirst. She ripped at her hair, screaming in pain, her tail snagged in the spinning fronds.

Sylla's message, ripped by the wreckage, fell into the sea below.

Seventeen

Tarian

Jake broke through to the surface. It was littered with scraps of kelp and splinters of wood. He looked for Cal. A hand grabbed his foot and she bobbed up beside him, her face scratched and hair specked with green.

'Where is it?' she said desperately. 'The message – can you see it?'

They scanned the water together, silently.

'We've got to find it!' Cal turned tail and Jake, still catching his breath, took one more gulp and dived after her.

Jake swept left and right. His keen eye caught by every flashing fin. Cal streaked past him, her hair flaming like a comet's tail. 'It must have got caught up in the paddywreck,' she told herself. 'If the seabed is sandy we might find it.'

However, to Cal's dismay, the seabed beneath them was covered with thick tufts of purple coral weed that stretched as far as the eye could see.

Still, they began to hunt, prodding and peering, agitating pipefish and stirring up clouds of feathery fronds.

The weed itself was slippery and the rock beneath crisscrossed with deep hidden fissures. Jake soon found it was too dangerous to stand on so he had to keep swimming. After what seemed like hours his arms and legs began to ache.

'It's no good,' he said dejectedly, 'this is hopeless. The message is probably torn to shreds. It would have slipped into this weed or dropped between the rocks. We'll never find it.'

After all the years she'd longed to know about her mother Cal couldn't accept that the precious cloth with its untold secrets was gone. 'It has to be here,' she muttered as she continued to skim the coral, 'we've just got to keep looking. I don't care how long it takes – it's close, I know it . . .'

Jake abandoned his search and felt around cautiously for a safe place to rest. He watched Cal desperately rake through the weed for a hint of silver thread. Suddenly, she stopped, 'Someone's coming,' she said. 'Listen . . .'

Jake was becoming accustomed to the cries and whistles of sea creatures, the plaintive moans that echoed through the water, but now he heard something different. From the distant haze, tinged with purple light reflected off the rocks, came a dull hammering and a clatter. It was growing louder. Moving nearer.

'Bloodfin?' Jake started.

'I don't know,' said Cal, puzzled. The sound was oddly familiar but she couldn't think why. 'There's nowhere to hide here. Let's go.'

She flung out her arms and soared up towards the surface. Jake followed but he couldn't match her speed. When Cal paused to wait for him, a look of astonishment flashed across her face. He turned too and saw the source of the strange sound. Travelling towards them was the most extraordinary caravan – first came two striped sailfish, swimming side by side, with long, lean bodies, blue backs, white bellies and slender sickle-shaped tails. Their spears reminded Jake of the deadly marlin. As if of one mind, the sailfish raised their broad fins which fluttered like ragged flags. Each wore a harness around its body from which trailed a dozen or more lengths of rope and chain. On to these were tied an assortment of objects; scraps of metal, a small broken propeller, a crook of bone that might have been the jaw of a young whale, empty lobster pots and net bags filled with urchins and molluscs. They banged and clattered together. Both harnesses were attached to a pair of reins and holding these, following the sailfish, was a Delphine man swimming powerfully through the water.

This man was quite unlike the Bloodfin Jake had seen. He had loose, white hair and stubble on his jaw. His body was thin but immensely strong and wiry. Jake noticed how every muscle and sinew strained as he controlled the will of the big fish. He wore a curious wristband of twisted wire with green glass beads and there were scars on his forearms and chest. From his shoulders flowed a layered cloak made with scraps of fishing net laced together.

He reminded Jake of a picture in Charley's big Bible, of a bare-chested old man on a mountaintop, looking up at jagged lightning in a thundery sky. Jake couldn't decide if he was young and strong with the appearance of age or an old man who had somehow retained his vigour.

'Look,' said Cal, 'on his belt – the chain of keys.' It was Tarian, the trader.

Tarian slowed as he came near. He pulled hard on the reins to halt the big fish, but they tugged resentfully, smashing their cargoes against each other, so that he had to wrench their leashes to bring them to rest. Then he turned and looked directly at Jake and Cal circling in the water above. He waited, watching them.

'Come on,' said Cal. 'He may have seen the message.'

Jake swam cautiously alongside Cal and felt the water constrict around them. The sailfish nosed the weed impatiently, still straining at their reins.

They approached Tarian. He stared with silent fascination at Jake, his emerald eyes glinting from their deep sockets like fugitive creatures in dark caves.

'I come from the Silvertail village,' Cal began, 'my name is—'

'I know who you are,' interrupted Tarian in a low, quiet voice. 'You are Pelin's daughter. Pelin the Sorrowful.'

Cal was taken aback to hear her father called by this name.

'There was a raid,' she said. 'Bloodfin attacked our village. There's no one left . . . Just us.'

If Tarian was listening he showed no sign of it. He studied Jake's legs and feet, his unwebbed hands. Jake tried to tread water but he felt embarrassed by his awkward movements. 'Don't flinch, you idiot,' he told himself. 'Let him look at you.' As he met Tarian's gaze Jake had the odd sensation that Tarian was looking right through him. He lifted his chin defiantly.

'I'm searching for news of my father,' Cal persisted. 'I know he escaped . . . I'm sure he did.'

'I have many eyes and ears,' said Tarian, turning to her at last. 'I know much. But knowledge is powerful currency. You wish to learn about the fate of your father. Show me first what you know. Have you learnt how to breathe life into the drowned?'

'I'm not drowned,' Jake blurted. The sailfish bridled at the sound of his voice. Tarian tugged their reins. 'And her name is Cal.'

'He's a Creeper, but he can breathe like us,' said Cal. Tarian pondered on this, leaving a long silence that Cal felt compelled to break. 'My mother—'

'Ah, yes . . .' Tarian sighed.

Suddenly, a sheet of darkness gathered above their heads. All three felt a chill flood through their veins.

Jake and Cal were seized with alarm. How could they have forgotten to watch for the Bloodfin! They looked up, but the dark shape immediately fled.

'Treacherous shadows,' muttered Tarian. 'Come. A malevolent current is swelling . . .' The agitated sailfish pulled hard, eager to move off. 'We cannot talk here.'

Eighteen

Gifts

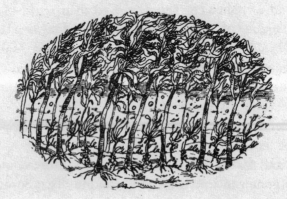

Tarian held out a rein to Jake. 'Hold this.'

Jake hesitated, wary of the muscle power on the other end. 'Hold it. You'll never keep up with those!' He gestured at Jake's legs and a smirk crossed his face.

Jake looked to Cal for assurance and she gave him an encouraging nod. He took hold of the reins. His hands seemed tiny beside Tarian's fist. Jake braced himself but the sailfish pulled forward at a slow, smooth pace. Cal was immediately at his side.

'Where are we going?' she asked.

'Home,' said Tarian. 'It's been a long time.'

Before long Jake and Cal found themselves approaching

Tarian's scrapyard once more. Jake looked around nervously for Tangler. They came to the sandy clearing before the wrecked submarine. Tarian swung round abruptly and Jake dropped the reins, tumbling onto his back.

Sail Fish

'Watch out!' The chains of salvage hurtled across the sand, towards him. Cal dived at Jake and pushed him out of the way.

The sound of their arrival brought Tangler from the hatch. He almost fell down the side of the sub in his excitement and galloped towards them.

As Tarian unbuckled the reins Tangler greeted him with a hard slap, almost knocking him off balance.

'Hello, old friend,' chuckled Tarian and he returned the blow.

Spotting the chains, the octopus began to gather in the twisted metal and pots, keeping a wary distance from the sailfish.

Then Tangler caught sight of Cal and Jake. Holding the things he'd collected close to his body, he whipped another tentacle towards Jake, grabbed him by the ankle and dangled him upside down.

'Let go of me!' Jake pummelled him with his fists.

'Drop him,' Tarian growled at once.

For the second time Jake fell with a thud. Tangler moved off in a sulk.

'Don't mind him,' said Tarian. 'He's strong but he won't harm you.'

'Well, he stole something from us and nearly killed Cal,' said Jake, rubbing his sore elbow.

'And what did you have worth stealing?' asked Tarian.

Jake noticed a light in his eye. 'Come, let's eat and then we shall talk.'

Cal and Jake followed Tarian around the submarine to a tent-like shelter built against the far side. Tarian threw down the sailfish reins and disappeared into the sub through a wide gash in the metalwork hung with a curtain of net.

'I don't like him,' hissed Jake.

'But he knew my father,' said Cal. She felt uncomfortable about Tarian too. If he did know anything about her father – or mother – she was sure he wouldn't give his information freely.

Jake wandered round the shelter, which was scattered with more salvage: barrels of small engine parts, heaps of rope, coins and cutlery. Jake picked up an old sandglass. It reminded him of Lil's egg timer.

'What does he do with all this stuff?' he asked.

'He cleans it up and trades it,' Cal replied. 'We use *parr* to preserve Creeper things. It comes from whale tears.' She rubbed her thumb and forefinger together absently, remembering the waxy texture of a smudge of parr her father had once given her.

'How do you get that?'

'You can only collect it at a whale gathering. He probably trades in that too.' Cal took the sandglass from Jake and studied it. 'Creeper things have always fascinated our people,' she murmured. Jake watched her stroke the brass fittings as she turned the sandglass in her hands. Once more he recalled the face from his dream. The face of his mother. Their mother.

'Do you look like her . . . like Sylla?' he said, blushing as he realised he'd given away his thought.

'My father never told me, not really,' she replied softly. 'I wish I knew. He just couldn't bear to talk about her. He must have missed her so much.'

'You too – you've missed her, haven't you?'

Cal twitched her tail back and forth in the sand. 'Yes,' she said shyly. She had never spoken of it to anyone. 'I left home to find out about Sylla. I had so many questions. I just couldn't bear not knowing any more. Father didn't want me to go and we argued. But if I hadn't gone, if I hadn't found you, I would have never read that message. I can't believe we lost it! Can you remember any of it now? There was something about a Merrow breath and a gift, she said. Til's gift.'

Jake scratched his head. 'There *was* a gift . . . and she was going to find it safe keeping,' he said, 'because you were too young. I know – she called it your birthright.'

A loud clatter echoed inside the sub.

'Tarian knew my father, maybe he knew our mother too,' said Cal. 'Maybe he can help us,'

Jake scrambled close to Cal. 'No,' he said firmly. 'Don't tell him about the message. Don't tell him anything. This thing Sylla hid, you've got to keep it secret. If it's valuable someone like him – a trader – might want it.'

Cal hadn't considered this, but before she could speak Tarian emerged from the submarine carrying a large lumpy bundle wrapped in brown wrack. Jake gave Cal a stern look and she met his eye with a reluctant nod. Tarian placed the bundle down on a flat-topped rock where it fell open and a feast of shellfish and knotted twists of weed tumbled out.

Cal picked up a stub of yellow and crimson leaves bound together. 'What are these?' she asked. 'I've never seen them before.'

'Comb fans,' said Tarian, gesturing at the brightly coloured heap, 'urchins, slipweed, bursters, oysters, and pollyfish eggs.' He grunted with satisfaction at the sight. Then, without speaking further, settled himself down beside the rock table, lying on his side, propped up on an elbow, and began to eat. Jake and Cal did the same, glancing at each other occasionally, both taking the chance to think once more of what the message had told them.

The meal continued in silence. The food was tasty and Cal wondered where Tarian had travelled to find it. But oysters were her favourite. Seeing a big one she reached across the table. Suddenly Tarian raised himself and grabbed her hand. In an instant there was a flash of light as his other hand sliced the water with a shiny dagger. Jake leapt to his feet and knocked the knife out of Tarian's hand. It spun on to the sand.

For a moment no one moved. Then Tarian spoke.

'Take it,' he said, with a half smile, placing Cal's hand gently on the table, 'unless you can open an oyster with those Creeper hands?'

Jake cursed silently. He'd made an idiot of himself again. 'I thought,' he mumbled, 'I was afraid—'

'Yes,' said Tarian, 'you were afraid, but not for yourself. For her. Why should she need your protection I wonder? What should she fear?' Tarian picked up the dagger slowly, took the oyster Cal had been reaching for and began to prise it open. He beckoned for Jake to sit once more. 'I saw you back there long before you heard me,' he continued, breaking the shell apart with a gentle crack. 'I could feel your desperation. You are searching for something,' he offered the oyster to Cal, 'Something necessary, something vital. It must be of great value indeed.'

Cal took the oyster from him. His eyes met hers and revealed instantly that he knew many things. That he had more to tell. Cal wanted to trust Tarian, but she felt numbed by the water that moved around him. Her instinct, like all those who lived in the sea, was to be guided by its fluid truth. The water never lied. But she couldn't read it near him. It was curiously slack, streamy, without definition – as if he made no impression in it, gave nothing away.

Tarian turned to Jake who was looking at the knife. Its handle was inlaid with ivory and the blade itself appeared as bright and sharp as new. It was a fine weapon.

Jake remembered the Bloodfin spears. He and Cal had nothing to defend themselves with. He'd be a fool not to take it.

'What do you want for it?' Jake asked. Tarian held it out to him.

'You've already given me much,' he said, 'more than you intended, maybe.' He gestured at the salvage scattered around. 'These things you see are all base merchandise. There is far more vital trade in *knowledge*. Knowledge is power. See the beasts there—' he pointed to the sailfish cruising like sentinels around the sandy clearing '—those sails of theirs are gathering knowledge. Every swell, every current pulses with information. Those snouts of theirs smell threat, they smell fear. And these ears of mine hear secret, unspoken things.'

Jake was reminded of Batesy, the blind man who sat at the bar of the Anchor Inn day and night. He could hear unspoken things, so people said – like the cry of the catch tumbling in the nets far out at sea. 'Plenty of herring for supper,' Batesy would mutter. He was never wrong.

'The knife is fairly exchanged, Creeper boy.' Tarian put it firmly into Jake's hand. 'Just remember: show wisdom in how you use it – knowledge *and* knife.' With that he swam around the nose of the submarine, out of sight.

Jake took Cal's arm. 'Let's get away from here,' he said.

'No! Not yet!' she gripped his hand tight. 'I have to ask him about Sylla.'

But Cal didn't have to ask Tarian about Sylla. He returned, almost immediately, carrying a large nautilus shell, the size of a skull, striped with a sunset of gold, purple and pink. Cal had never seen such a beauty.

Tarian put the shell into her arms.

'You want to know about your father. I have been long away in Jade Turtle Valley and beyond, where this Bloodfin terror is yet unknown. I have heard nothing of Pelin.'

Her heart jolted, as if in that one beat it had turned to stone.

Tarian lifted Cal's face gently. 'But your mother – she came here once, long ago.' He paused and his expression softened. 'She was fading, dying, but even then her beauty persisted.'

'Why did she come?' Jake asked as he saw Cal was unable to speak, blinking back her tears.

'She wanted a vessel. A shell. What could she need it for, so near the end?' Again he looked deep into Cal's eyes. They glazed with a trance-like expression. Tarian stared deeper. 'I see the face of Sylla, I see her spirit in you. Why did she want the shell?'

Cal stuttered. 'I think she wanted to – to—'

Jake interrupted. 'How could she know?' He moved in front of Cal to break Tarian's gaze. 'She was a baby. She doesn't remember her mother.'

Tarian clicked his tongue. 'Secrets and shadows. Both dissolve away.'

Cal recovered herself. 'Please tell me,' she asked, 'did you give her a shell?'

'You hold his brother in your hands,' replied Tarian.

'But this is promised to another.' Without a further word he took the nautilus shell from Cal and wrapped his cloak around it.

Suddenly an avalanche of rocks tumbled down the cliff at the edge of the clearing. Sand and rubble billowed up, scattering dozens of crabs and a pair of startled triggerfish. Tangler shot out of a dark hole nearby and in a twitch the sailfish dashed after him. In the same instant Tarian was gone, swimming up the cliff face to investigate the rock fall, the nautilus still in his arms.

'Now's our chance,' said Jake. 'Let's get out of here.'

This time Cal didn't object. She darted into the clearing, flipped a somersault as if to shake herself free of Tarian's sway and followed Jake into the scrapyard maze.

When Tarian returned some time later the sailfish were nowhere to be seen. Tangler slouched in the shadow of the sub, rubbing some rubyweed into a wound in his trunk. Tarian inspected the gash.

'You'll live,' he said dismissively.

Tangler lashed out but Tarian caught the end of the tentacle in his fist.' Where's the Creeper?' he asked. 'Where did they go? 'Tangler pulled away from him.

'Listen to me . . .' Tarian spoke softly. 'One will come, of our kind but not of our kind. He shall be called the Tide Turner.' His eyes flashed. 'What power is that! You must find the boy. Come, I will instruct you . . .'

Reluctantly, Tangler followed Tarian into the sub.

Nineteen

Big Enough to Swallow Mountains

Cal found a swift undertow to carry them away from Tarian's place. The force dragged them along at great speed but Jake struggled to keep his balance and was buffeted against the seabed. He soon needed to rest. He grabbed Cal's wrist. She understood at once and pulled him free.

They made for an outcrop of rocks, thick with furbelows, and found a shallow trench, just big enough to conceal them both.

'So, what next?' said Jake, rubbing his bruises.

'I don't know,' sighed Cal. 'None of the Silvertail settlements are safe if the Bloodfin are hunting us down. I hope Skimmer reached the nearest pod with my warning in time. If only he'd come back.'

Jake fingered the nugget of glass, still in his pocket. 'What about Sylla's message? Let's try and remember more. What was all that stuff about the breath?'

The channel of water about them heaved suddenly, as if drawing itself to Jake's words. 'The breath was important . . . Sylla called it a gift,' said Cal.

'And Aran, the sister, said it was her inheritance.'

'Do you think that's the birthright – the breath? Did she mean the Merrow breath?' Cal flicked her tail excitedly. 'Of course – it was passed from mother to daughter. That's what Sylla wanted to give me!'

Jake was still puzzled. 'But she felt she had to hide it, for safekeeping—' He was sure he was missing something obvious. Then it came to them both at the same time.

'Tarian's shell!'

'Sylla hid the breath in the nautilus shell and you have to find it,' cried Jake.

'*We* have to find it,' said Cal. 'She wanted us to do this together. I'm sure of it. That's the reason only you could open the box. You must help me.'

'I don't expect I'll be much help,' said Jake. 'I slow you down. I may be able to breathe like you, but I don't have your strength. I'm not one of your kind.'

Jake's words struck Cal like a lighthouse bell. The prophecy. The Tide Turner. Yes, he was of her kind yet not of her kind. But what did it mean? She took him by the shoulders.

'Jake – you have Delphine blood,' she said, 'don't you feel it yet? Who knows how much of our nature flows through you. Trust the sea. You are strong and you could learn to use your body, to read the water like us.'

Jake knew he had changed. He wasn't the boy who'd sat alone in his boat such a short time ago. And he wanted to learn more. He wanted to feel what she felt. 'Yes, I'll help,' he said, 'until I start holding you back.'

'Good!' Cal squeezed his hand. 'So?' She looked at him expectantly. 'Where did Sylla put the shell? Where would you put something you wanted to hide?'

Jake picked up an empty dogwhelk and a tiny prawn toppled out of it. 'You'd put it where no one can see it.' He looked out beyond their rocky sanctuary into the boundless green water. 'The sea's big enough to swallow mountains,' Lil used to say, 'just like your appetite!' How would they ever find one shell in that vast ocean?

'We could never search every cave and crevice,' sighed Cal. 'Anyway, it's so beautiful – it might have been found already. If Sylla didn't trust my father to know about it she wouldn't have left a guardian.'

Jake agreed.

Cal shut her eyes. Her head had started to throb. Suddenly her aimless search had a purpose, the hope of answers, of Sylla's gift – but how to begin? 'If only we had Skimmer,' she said again. 'Shall I take a chance and call him?'

'What about the Bloodfin? What if they're near?'

'We need to move fast,' said Cal, 'and we'll have no chance of escape without him.' Jake saw it was a grim risk they had to take. He nodded and gripped the hilt of Tarian's knife.

Cal slipped into a clearing and beat rhythmically with her tail. Then she dashed back into the trench with Jake and they stared silently into the distance . . .

Nothing came but an inquisitive seal and a dory stalking a little fish. Still they peered into the dimming water. Jake's eyelids grew heavy. He felt an overwhelming desire to nestle against the weed and sleep.

'Maybe Skimmer's waiting until dark,' whispered Cal.

'Maybe,' said Jake, wondering what else was out there, able to rely on sound and taste and smell in the night water. 'We can't see anything much now.' He yawned. 'Let's get some rest and start looking in the morning.'

But Cal continued to listen, straining every nerve to identify the minute movements of creatures flitting and floating around them. At last, exhausted, she gave up her watch. Jake was already curled against the rock. Cal studied him in the weak light. His will was strong but his Delphine instincts so new. She lay down beside him. What was the fate of this brother-kin? What other surprises might Sylla's message have revealed? Could they really find the last Merrow breath and turn the treacherous currents around them?

Cal clutched Sylla's pendant and, as stillness settled, she fell asleep herself.

Twenty

Star Fall

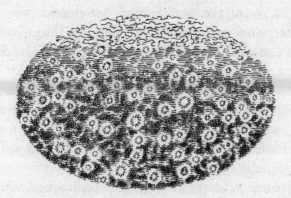

J ake woke up with a jerk and slapped his leg hard. Ugh! Something had snaked across his calf. He sat up.

It was still dark. Jake felt gingerly about, but found nothing lurking nearby. With a shudder he lay back against the rock and tried to make himself comfortable again. The water lapped his body soothingly. Maybe he'd been dreaming after all.

But Jake couldn't get back to sleep. He felt uneasy. He looked deeper into the darkness and could just make out the form of Cal's sleeping body not far from his feet. Yet they were not alone, he knew it.

Then, as Jake's eyes became accustomed to the gloom, he

saw it wasn't utterly dark after all. Countless specks of light were slowly sinking through the blackness beyond. Tiny white moons and stars fluttered down as if the glittering night was falling from the sky. Jake was mesmerised. It seemed to him that the whole universe, heaven itself, was tumbling silently into the sea. He rose and made his way towards it.

Jake was drawn through the water as if still asleep, hardly aware of his own motion. He passed beyond the rocks into more open water and there, as if stepping into a snowfall, he came among them: millions of minute, delicate creatures, like ghostly glass insects, their transparent bodies lit by splinters of moonlight as they descended through the dark. Some were like tiny centipedes, others miniature shrimp and jellyfish, paddling, pulsing, wriggling their antennae, trailing thread-like tentacles. Those that fell close towards him darted away.

Jake swung his arms around him and laughed. For some inexplicable reason he felt immensely happy. He swam further, on and on, sharing the secret night dance, pausing to twist and somersault like an acrobat.

'I can fly!' he cried. 'I can fly!'

After some time Jake sank to the seabed, still laughing, shaking the living confetti from his hair. He looked around once more. The water was clearing now. The creatures began to disperse and faint morning light was penetrating the darkness. All of a sudden, Jake realised he had no idea where he was. He started to his feet but a forceful swell knocked him down again. He was completely lost! Panic ran through him like an electric shock. In an instant Jake realised the horror of his situation: lost in the sea, where only one person in the world cared whether he existed at all;

lost in a sea of haunting shadows, murderous marlin and worse, somewhere out there, Bloodfin, sent to hunt him down.

'Keep calm,' he said. 'Think clearly, now . . .'

Cal had said he was meant to be there. He had something important to do. He remembered her words about 'reading the water'. Maybe the water can tell me something, he thought, help me find my way back.

Not knowing what to hope for, Jake sat still and steadied himself. He shut his eyes, stretched out his arms and concentrated on the fluid movement around him. At first he was distracted by his clothes flapping against his body and his hair floating around his head. Then a starfish grabbed one of Jake's toes and broke his concentration. He shook it off and began again.

Nothing. He remained motionless, receptive, waiting for something meaningful. Still nothing. He tried once more, urgently now, desperately . . .

A chilly stream rippled across the seabed. As it passed, an odd sensation crept over him: a tangy, salty sensation, as though he were actually tasting the water through his skin, all over his body. The feeling was alarming and unpleasant. It sharpened, drenching him with a bitter, stinging wave. Jake began to tremble uncontrollably. His skin felt raw, as if some protective layer had dissolved. What was happening? He tried to keep a grip on himself and stay focused. 'Learn this,' he told himself, 'remember this . . .'

Suddenly the sea heaved into him and a biting acid blast shot across Jake's back.

'Cal!' he screamed and, kicking off the sandbed, swam as fast as he could away from the source of the pain.

Twenty-one

Deep and Dark

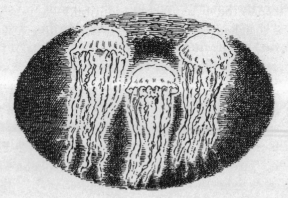

Cal raced through the water using all her Delphine skill to navigate at speed through unfamiliar terrain. She beat her tail frantically. Jake's panic had electrified the water. Why had he left the safety of the trench? How could she have slept so deeply? His fear had woken her – had it also signalled his whereabouts to the Bloodfin?

Then she heard Jake's scream. Too late! However, to her relief he appeared, moments later, swimming desperately towards her.

'Where have you been? What happened?'

Jake threw himself at her, shaking and pale. They dived

down and collapsed on the sand, scattering spider crabs into the weed. At first he couldn't speak. Cal shook him.

'What happened?' she repeated.

'I saw something – something wonderful,' he gasped at last. 'All these tiny things, floating down like snowflakes . . .'

'Snowflakes?' Cal looked anxiously around. 'What's snowflakes?'

Jake laughed. 'There were tiny creatures, all swirling down through the water. It was beautiful.'

'Oh,' Cal sighed with relief, 'the Dawn Falling.' She let go her grip of him.

'What was it?' asked Jake.

'It happens every night. When darkness comes, small creatures rise to feed near the surface – we call that the Dusk Rising,' Cal explained. 'Then just before the Golden Eye opens they sink down again – that's the Dawn Falling.'

Jake had hardly noticed morning arrive. He looked about now. Veils of light, the colour of spring wood-land, slanted through the water. A shoal of hungry mackerel shot swiftly overhead hunting for breakfast, their bellies flashing like bright blades. Three pearly jellyfish ballooned towards the surface, trailing their tentacles behind them. Exotic turquoise sea slugs am-bled over pillows of puffball sponges and anemones opened and stretched their arms. Everywhere creatures were stirring. Cal handed him a burster. It tasted good.

Jellyfish

'The Dawn Falling is beautiful,' Cal continued. 'You should have woken me. But what frightened you? What made you scream?'

Jake rubbed his arms.

'I was lost,' he said. 'It was dark.'

'You could have called,' said Cal. 'I'll always hear you.'

'I didn't want to,' Jake hesitated, 'in case the Bloodfin heard – but then I did call anyway, didn't I? I couldn't stop myself.'

Cal saw he was afraid.

'Will they find us now?'

She tried to muster a reassuring smile. 'Let's go up to the Overbreath,' she said. 'You need some air.'

Jake welcomed the chance to swim towards the light. Grabbing a fistful of red seaweed to chew, they made their way to the surface. As they swam Jake told Cal about his attempt to read the water.

'That's what sent you back to me!' said Cal. 'You were feeling your own fear in the water. It must have been terrifying.'

'It was painful.' Jake winced. His skin was still sore.

'The Sea Spirit used your fear to direct you.'

'What's the Sea Spirit?'

'She's our creator, the pulse of our lifeflow – and yours too. Everything comes from the Sea Spirit . . .'

Before Jake had time to ask more they both surfaced, breaching the crisp, blue morning in an explosion of sun-shot spray. Jake floated in the water, blinking at the bright light and gulping down the brisk air. Cal immediately arched her back, dived down again and re-emerged, fast this time, leaping in a long low arc across the glimmering sea. A curtain of water cascaded from her body, shimmering with tiny rainbows. Down she plunged, then up once more, trailing wisps of spindrift. Cal loved the freedom she felt when she leapt out of the sea, the lightness as the water fell from her limbs – it was like flying out of her own skin. Then she loved the shock on impact as she dived from air to ocean at rapid speed. Best of all was one after the other, over and over, water and air, water and air . . .

Jake watched her jealously, but with some pride that such an astonishing creature should be his own sister. He could still hardly believe it.

As before, the fresh, invigorating breath made him light-headed for a while. This time they were far from the shore. A tiny white sail moved slowly towards the horizon but the land was nothing more than a smudge of grey beyond it. He saw the moon still hanging around in the morning sky as if reluctant to pass on.

'Where do all those creatures in the Dawn Falling go?' asked Jake when Cal returned, bright-eyed, to his side.

'They hide deep down where it's dark,' she replied.

Jake and Cal looked at each other with the same instant thought.

'That's it!' Cal smashed both her arms down on the water, showering Jake.

'Hey!'

'That's it! In the dark – that's where you'd hide something. Listen,' she said excitedly, 'Tarian said Sylla was very weak when she left him, so she must have needed to find a hiding place close by. There's a deep undersea cavern called the Serpent's Throat – not far from Tarian's place. It's very dangerous. If my father knew about it Sylla might have known it too. When I was young I begged him to take me. He always refused. But when he saw how determined I was he finally agreed. I think he was afraid I'd go looking for it myself.' Cal realised with shame how her father could not trust her.

'What's it like?' asked Jake.

'Well, I didn't go right into the Serpent's Throat itself,' said Cal. 'First we passed through a maze of rocks called Fang Gully – a big anglerfish led us through. Then we came to Gaping Craw, a huge cave, the biggest I've ever seen, and there, at the far end, was a black hole – that was the entrance to the Serpent's Throat.'

Jake shuddered. The thought of the Serpent's Throat filled him with dread. And how would they find anything in the dark?

A wheeling gull caught the sun on its white breast. A wisp of cloud drifted across the empty blue sky.

'All right.' He breathed deeply, wishing he could take the light into his body as well as air. 'We've no other idea of where to look. Let's go.'

Far below them a dark shape shadowed their sun-bathed silhouettes . . .

Twenty-two

Ravine

Jake was silent as they swam to the Serpent's Throat. He noticed how Cal never stopped looking above and below them. Often she slowed and circled nervously, listening, feeling the flow. He was sure that Sylla had wanted him to protect his sister, but how? Should he try to read the water again? His experience after the Dawn Falling had frightened him. No, he decided. I'll watch and wait. Trust the water, that's what Cal had said. If it was right for him to be there he would find his way.

The seabed sloped steeply and folded itself into a valley of crimped rock studded with dead man's fingers and clumps of rust beltstrap weed. The water grew cold and cloudy. As they swam further Cal and Jake could see less and less through the gloom. Indistinct shapes drifted around them.

Cal slowed down. 'Stay close.'

She wondered whether they were doing the right thing. Would Sylla have hidden something so precious in the Serpent's Throat? It seemed a desperate place to go when she was weak and alone. Cal thought again of her mother's message. What could they be sure of from the fragment she'd read? Cal had always assumed the Merrows were creatures of myth. It was incredible to discover they were real after all. But had Sylla, her own mother, really been one of them? Would that mean Cal was the last now – the last Merrow in the whole ocean – for ever?

If that was true, the survival of the ancient powers was in her hands. The chilling curse of Sylla's sister rang through Cal's head. Maybe she was still alive, out there, among the shadows that seemed to follow them . . . searching for that breath herself? *We have to find the shell,* Cal pleaded silently, *before Aran finds it, before the Bloodfin murder more Silvertails, before they hunt us down.* The sea had never felt so cold, so hostile, so dangerous . . .

Cal fingered Sylla's pendant hanging around her neck. She held it to her lips. 'Help me,' she muttered. 'Help us both.'

Cal was so lost in her thoughts she didn't notice the valley narrow and deepen, but Jake was alarmed to see the rock walls rise steeply around them and a ravine gape open beneath. A stinging wave of fear smacked his body as before.

'It's not safe here,' cried Jake. 'Can't you feel it?' But his warning came too late.

Like bats from a cave at dusk, a horde of Bloodfin burst from the dark chasm. They sliced, fast and furious, through the water, swooped, looped and attacked from all directions.

Cal screamed.

'Hold on!' Jake grabbed her and pulled her close. 'Don't let go.'

One after another the Bloodfin charged towards Cal and Jake, their eyes burning red with menace. They dived from above, exploded from below in a volley of bubbles, skimmed broadside and buzzed them from behind. Cal and Jake were being herded, trapped in an invisible cage. In terror Cal struggled and beat Jake's leg with her tail, but he didn't let her go. Faster and closer the Bloodfin whipped the water around them, tightening it like a tourniquet. Cal thought she would faint. Then just as it seemed the water would wring the breath from them both the Bloodfin began circling, slow and wide. The spinning swell subsided. Jake steadied his dizzy head and counted seven of them. He fought hard not to retch at their rank, oily stench. The Bloodfin were young but their faces contorted with ugly scowls. Jake guessed they were a gang but there seemed no obvious leader.

Warily they closed in again, pushing and shoving each other, gripping the hilts of the metal blades that hung from belts around their trunks. They were fascinated, like Tarian, by Jake's legs. He kicked out at them. A youth with a gruesome scab across his eye made a grab for Jake's ankle but, instantly, a fist smashed down upon his wrist.

'Leave it!' snarled the Bloodfin beside him. 'This is the freak we were sent for. He must be the one.' His words gave Cal an idea, a desperate idea – but they had nothing to lose. She wrestled free of Jake.

'Keep away,' she cried, glaring at them one by one. 'This is the Tide Turner. See, he has come.'

In an instant the gang's fascination turned to fear. To Jake's amazement the Bloodfin backed off.

'What did you say?' hissed Jake. But Cal didn't answer. She clenched her fists and continued.

'He is the one – of our kind, but not of our kind.'

'Tide Turner?' A Bloodfin wearing a necklet of shark's teeth swam forward. He snarled at Cal. Jake grabbed her hand.

'That's no Tide Turner!' He spat at Jake. But he narrowed his eyes and peered at Jake's legs again closely.

'Try him,' said Cal, unflinching. Blood rushed around her head almost drowning her daring words.

Jake couldn't believe his ears – what was she doing?

'Take us up to the shallows!' said Cal.

She's trying to get us a chance to escape, Jake thought. I've got to help her. Suddenly he remembered Tarian's knife in his back pocket. He slipped his hand around his belt. 'Keep talking,' he urged Cal under his breath, but she gritted her teeth and fell silent, willing them with every nerve in her body to take a risk.

The gang gathered to talk in tense, agitated voices.

'Why should we take him back and hand him over? We found the freak, let's see what he can do.' A disagreement quickly erupted. One with a split fluke broke away and circled the group threateningly.

Jake's fingers reached the handle of the knife. Got it! He slid the blade out of his pocket and swung it around before him.

'Get away!' he yelled, stabbing the water fiercely. The Bloodfin reared back in surprise.

'I *am* the Tide Turner. You have no power over me.'

Cal squeezed his hand tight. Once more the Bloodfin backed off. Whoever this Tide Turner was, thought Jake, he had the power to scare them. But, in a flash, a chain lasso whipped through the water and knocked the knife from his hand. Jake lurched. Instantly a Bloodfin darted forward to catch the spinning knife. He grinned. The gang, bold again, crowded round to inspect it. Jake was furious. The knife snatcher, now taking the lead, gestured to the others to gather behind him. He approached Jake slowly, holding the knife to his face. Then he grabbed a fistful of Jake's hair and, with a jab of the blade, sliced it off. Jake clutched his head and kicked out again. The other Bloodfin smirked and darted to and fro, impressed.

'We'll take you up, Tide Turner,' the knife snatcher said, curling his thin lip. 'We know the legend. Maybe that's why we were sent to find you. But hunting would be easy with the tides in *our* power . . .'

The knife snatcher shoved his leathery, pockmarked face close. Jake had never seen eyes burn with such malice. 'But if you have no power at all, Creeper . . .' he opened his fist and let the locks of Jake's hair fall, 'we'll cut off your head too.' The rest of the gang sniggered. 'Take him,' he ordered, 'and chain her up.'

Twenty-three

Plague

The one-eyed Bloodfin grabbed Cal's arm and she screamed.

Jake lashed out.

Then darkness fell. Deafening screams ripped through the water and turmoil boiled around them. In the confusion Jake felt Cal pulled away from him.

Almost at once the darkness fractured and light broke through again. A vast swarm of fat venom slugs had descended and smothered the Bloodfin. They clamped themselves to their victims, stabbing them with thorny spines and sucked at the wounds, oozing poison into the punctured flesh. The Bloodfin yelled in agony and smashed their fists against their own writhing skin.

Jake looked desperately for Cal. To his relief he saw she was unharmed below him, buffeted by the churning water, watching the frenzied attack with horror.

'Aieee, coaco!' An eerie cry pierced the chaos.

Immediately the slugs released their victims and gathered in the dense cloud that had cast darkness over them all moments before.

The Bloodfin fled up the ravine.

Jake and Cal turned. Out of the murky haze floated a massive, ragged sphere. The vicious plague swam directly towards it. Cal and Jake felt the water contract as the shape moved closer and then, from its heart they heard a shrill voice.

'Come, little ones, come.'

Twenty-four

Protection

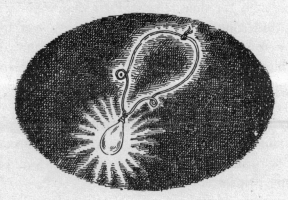

Orcara propelled her vast kelpish body through the ravine, pulsing like a green jellyfish. She carried the narwhal staff with her conger eel twisted possessively around it.

'Come, come.' She flicked a crooked finger and beckoned impatiently. The swarming slugs enveloped her and burrowed themselves deep in her shroud of rotting weed.

Orcara nodded with satisfaction, gnawing her white gums in an undisguised sneer.

'So, we meet again,' she said, gesturing with her staff for Cal and Jake to draw close. 'I find you far from safety.'

Orcara put her thin lips to the eel's head, almost nibbling

some secret instruction into its skull. It slithered off the staff and away to the depths of the ravine below.

'They would have killed us,' said Cal, still reeling.

'Yes,' said Jake, 'you were just in time, I mean they – your—' He fell silent. Orcara grunted an acknowledgement. 'You left me a warning at Strapkelp,' she said, 'so now I have come to save you. How fortunate I was collecting spinweed nearby. And the ankle?' She pointed to Jake's leg.

'Yes, it's strong, thank you.'

'We were lost,' said Cal. 'It was stupid to come this way.'

'Let me take you home,' hissed Orcara. 'I am travelling to Silvertail waters. There is much healing to be done there. The Bloodfin won't harm you while you are in my care.'

'Have there been more attacks?' asked Cal.

'Evil tides are gathering strength. Powerful tides that cannot be turned . . .' She eyed Jake intently. 'You'd be wise to accept my protection.'

Cal thought of the Bloodfin with dread. Were they the only ones she had to fear? Orcara had helped them twice now, maybe she could help them find the shell – and soon, before it was too late. 'We're not going back,' Cal said. 'We're searching for something.'

'Searching?' Orcara fussed at her kelp fronds, picking at a string of crab claws woven there. 'What could possibly entice you to these dismal waters?'

'Nothing,' interrupted Jake, alarmed at Cal's words. 'Nothing. She wanted to show me a cave, that's all.'

'It's all right, Jake. We can tell her,' said Cal. 'Maybe we can't do this on our own.'

Once more Orcara set her eyes upon Jake. The crystal he'd been clutching in his pocket turned as cold as ice.

'I'll help you,' she said, softening her gaze. 'You can trust me. I know these waters well, and have many at my call. My reach stretches far and wide.'

'But what about the Bloodfin?' Jake blurted out, confused. 'Why are they after me?'

'The Bloodfin are ruthless,' said Orcara. 'Fear is their weapon, but also their weakness. Like every wretched creature they fear what they do not understand – so they must destroy it.' She turned to Cal. 'You should have protection.' The tip of her solitary spike tooth peeped from her smile.

'She's got me,' said Jake. 'I'll look after her.'

Orcara flexed her fingers and her knuckles cracked like gunshot. Cal noticed the eel return and slither back beneath Orcara's shroud. She shuddered.

'Creeper,' said Orcara reproachfully, 'you cannot protect her – you know you are quarry yourself. Don't you feel it? Shadows are gathering, a powerful current stirs, raising creatures from the deep – creatures of eternal night, merciless demons with murkwater in their veins and stone in their hearts. Soon it will be strong enough to overwhelm the will of the Sea Spirit herself.' As she spoke Orcara seemed to swell, spreading her kelp like swaying tentacles around her. She turned to Cal and reached to stroke her hair. 'You are like me,' she said, '. . . destined to follow wayward drifts. Let me protect you. No one else can.'

How good it would be to feel safe, thought Cal. Orcara continued to stroke her hair and Cal's body felt strangely buoyant as if it was starting to float, shedding weight. If only she could share her fears, share the task her mother had given her . . .

A patch of numbness suddenly bit into Cal's throat. Her

pendant had turned to ice. Cal tugged it away from her skin. The touch of the crystal shook her from her swoon. She suddenly felt impatient to be away. They had to find Sylla's shell and find it fast.

'We owe you our lives and we're grateful,' Cal said, 'but the Creeper and I must go on alone. We don't need protection. We won't stray from lightwater.'

'As you wish, so it must be,' muttered Orcara, shaking her head. 'But I will hear your call. Remember, my reach is far and wide.'

Cal nodded to Jake. 'Come on, it's cold down here.' And with that she grabbed Jake's hand and swam upwards, pulling him beside her. 'Thank goodness,' he cried, 'I never want to go there again!'

Twenty-five

Legend

As soon as they were out of Orcara's sight Cal doubled back and took a wide arc to rejoin the ravine further along.

'You must be mad,' cried Jake as he realised what she was doing. 'I'm not going back there.' He pulled up short, treading water, and refused to go on.

'I think I *am* mad,' sighed Cal. She looped around him, 'But I know we can't give up. We have to find that shell. My father was worried about some danger waiting for me. And you heard Tarian and Orcara both talk about a dark current gathering force. We've both felt it, haven't we? Not just the Bloodfin – something has been following us, lurking, always hidden.'

'How can the shell help?' asked Jake, as confused as ever.

'It's the Merrow breath,' said Cal. 'I'm sure of it now. The Sea Spirit made the Merrows to protect the sea, to keep peace and harmony in the ocean. When Sylla died the last breath was lost. What if the protection was lost then too?'

Jake thought for a moment. 'You believe this dangerous force can only grow because the last of the Merrows is gone?'

'Yes,' said Cal. 'But if we can find the breath, we might restore the peace. Maybe it's the only chance. And that's why we're in danger; from those who want to rise against the Sea Spirit.'

'Do you think your father knew this?' asked Jake.

'He always said I wasn't like the others. I'm sure he guessed something,' said Cal. 'Maybe not all of Sylla's secret. I suppose I'll never know.' She swallowed hard. 'So you see I *must* find the shell. I'll have to go alone if you're afraid to.'

Jake thrashed his legs and punched the water.

'Well, I *am* afraid – and you should be.'

'Yes,' said Cal. 'I am. But I don't believe my mother would have done this without helping me somehow.'

Jake turned round and about in the water, deciding what to do. Then he remembered something that had puzzled him earlier. 'What about this Tide Turner? Even his name scared the Bloodfin. Can't he help us?'

Cal frowned.

'There's a prophecy that I heard long ago,' she said. 'Since I met you, since all this began, I can't stop thinking about it. The legend says there'll be a time when treachery flows through the sea. Then someone, of our kind but not of our kind, will come with the power to restore the peace. He'll be called the Tide Turner. I took a chance that the Bloodfin knew the legend too.'

'I don't understand,' Jake shook his head, trying to find some sense in this new riddle. 'Why were they afraid?'

Cal stared at him. 'Look at your legs, Jake. Look at you, down here with me—'

He gazed at her with a blank expression.

'Don't you see? They believed the Tide Turner was you. Maybe it *is*.'

Jake paused for a moment then darted to her side. 'What does it mean?' he repeated dumbly. 'Why didn't you tell me before? What is a Tide Turner?'

'I wish I understood myself,' said Cal. 'But no one else can help me, Jake. Only you. Whoever you really are. Whatever you are . . .'

Twenty-six

To the Serpent's Throat

Jake followed Cal back through the ravine, lost in thought. Daggers of rock rose from the black crevice below. They dived deeper.

Jake shivered. 'This water's freezing.'

'It's going to get colder,' Cal warned. 'This is Fang Gully.'

Sure enough Jake saw that the tapering blades were shaped like gigantic shark's teeth. Soon the fangs were twenty feet high.

A pair of marbled ling snaked ahead in the wake of a

small shoal of dogfish. A long, mournful groan reverberated through the water from the great throat of a whale far away in the open ocean. Jake listened for an answering call, but none came.

'Stop a minute,' he said. 'We've got to mark our way or we'll be lost down here for ever.' He looked around and saw a funnel-like object sticking out of the sand. Jake swam over and tugged at the rim. A shield-shaped piece of metal broke off in his hand.

'Perfect!' he said. With force he bent it double, then used the broken edge to scrape a patch of algae from the nearest rock. It left a chalky mark. 'We'll do this every few strokes to leave a trail.'

'What if the Bloodfin return and follow it?'

'They don't need a trail,' scowled Jake. 'They can smell us! Come on. Let's find this shell and get out of here as fast as we can.'

Presently the gully became so dense they could no longer see in any direction.

Cal called through the water as her father had done before. And, just as before, a hairy old anglerfish appeared.

Jake had never seen such a grotesque creature. It inspected him closely with tiny bead-like eyes buried deep in the flabby folds of its monstrous head. Its grey flesh was covered with ranks of long spines. But most alarming was the gawping pink, fat-lipped mouth, spiked with rows of needle sharp teeth. Above it dangled a glowing lure, a welcome to the jaws below . . .

The anglerfish turned away and began to progress slowly through the gully.

'It'll lead us to Gaping Craw,' hissed Cal. 'But don't follow too close.' Jake nodded. He had no intention of getting friendly with a fiendish looking creature like that, however obliging. As they went, swerving this way and that, he nicked the rocks with his makeshift blade.

The anglerfish was distracted by any passing creature that might fall prey to its lure. However, eventually they came to a clearing before a cliff. A sudden noise startled the anglerfish and it darted off. They were left alone. Before them was a narrow crack in the foot of the cliff, barely wider than Jake and not quite twice as tall.

'That's it,' said Cal, 'Gaping Craw.'

'Your father took you in *there*?' said Jake in disbelief.

'He wasn't going to,' admitted Cal, 'but he stooped down to look at an injured starfish and I slid in. So he had to follow.'

Jake smiled at her determination.

'I'll go first,' she said.

'No!' Jake looked around. 'No. I'll go first. We don't know what might be waiting for us inside.'

Clutching the metal shard and steeling his nerves Jake shuffled sideways through the crack in the rock.

The passageway was dark and cramped. He counted twenty paces through. When he emerged Jake found himself on a ledge, high in the wall of a vast cavern. He felt dizzy for a moment and steadied himself against the wall as he took in the sight. Thin columns of milky light fell from chimney holes in the roof. Above his head a canopy of tiny, lumines-cent creatures clung to the cave ceiling and glowing curtains of algae draped the walls and rocks below. The cavern was carpeted with pale moss weed. Drifts of white fungal forms grew through it, giving the appearance of a sickly forest floor. Cal was quickly at his side.

'There it is!' She pointed to a ring of jagged rocks in a small hollow at the foot of the far wall. In the midst of them was a black hole. 'The Serpent's Throat,' she whispered. 'Come on.'

Jake kicked off the ledge and swam with Cal through Gaping Craw. As they passed the pillars of light each one vibrated like a plucked harp string. Cal headed for a great buttress of rock that arched over the Serpent's Throat. There she stopped and began to sing her calling song once more. To Jake's astonishment a dozen small lantern fish swam out of the hollow, their tiny bodies glistening with light. They darted towards her. These were followed by several more, and more again until a shoal of fishes swam around Cal like a whirl of silvery, windblown leaves. Cal moved closer to Jake and the lantern fish surrounded him too.

'Now,' said Cal, her face eerily distorted by the moony light, 'are you ready?'

Twenty-seven

Skimmer

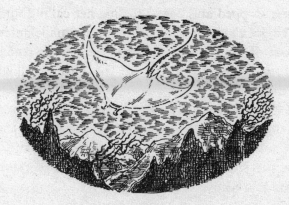

Skimmer coasted into Fang Gully. A long braid of knotted twine hung from his mouth. He glided among the sharp fins of rock, tipping his wings as he wheeled between them, searching for scent or sound.

Then he heard it – the familiar lilt of Cal's voice, echoing through the water ahead. With a surge of power he raced into the gully, tail straight as an arrow.

Skimmer navigated the maze skilfully. Within minutes he approached the clearing before the cliff.

Just as he slowed and unfurled his horns, something powerful struck his wing and thumped the base of his tail. Skimmer flipped awkwardly and crashed his other wing against a rock. A third blow behind his skull sent him flopping to the seabed.

Tangler picked up the braid that had fallen from Skimmer's mouth and tossed it away. He tugged at the ray's wing as if it were a plaything, but Skimmer lay lifeless, already half covered with settling sand.

Twenty-eight

Utter Darkness

The Serpent's Throat was a well of utter darkness. Even with the flotilla of lantern fish accompanying them, Jake and Cal could see nothing but blackness, thick as velvet. Cal reached for Jake's hand. They swam at a dreamlike pace.

'We need to reach the bottom,' she said in a hushed voice.

'How can we tell there aren't rocks ahead?' asked Jake. The disorientation quickly began to make him feel nauseous.

'Watch the lanterns,' said Cal. 'We're safe with them.'

Jake watched the little fish intently for any sudden evasive movement. The chill of the water seeped into his bones.

Down, down they sank. At last the lanterns spread out in

a fan shape. They had reached the bottom.

'It's bare rock!' cried Jake. He groped cautiously about. Some of the little fish followed his hand like an illuminated glove. 'There isn't a shell or a stone here – it's barren rock.' Then his foot hit something hard and smooth. Jake felt its curved surface with his toes. He turned and stretched out his glowing fingers towards it. 'This might be a shell . . .'

The curious lanterns flitted all over the round shape. Jake brushed them aside and a hollow-eyed skull stared blindly back.

'Ugh!' Cal and Jake shrank away.

'Let's get out of here,' said Cal. 'This can't be the place and Sylla couldn't have gone further if she was weak.' Jake heard a tremble in her voice. He drew her close. Once again the crystal in his pocket became icy cold. Jake took it out. 'Look at this . . .'

Cal peered in the dim light. Her necklace also stung with cold. She lifted it over her head and pulled it through her long hair.

'It's like mine.'

They held the two beside each other. Both were of the same aquamarine blue. Both tear-shaped. Jake's was scratched, but there was no doubt they belonged to each other. Gently Jake pushed the two tears together and they fitted snugly, making a complete crystal disc.

'It gets very cold sometimes,' said Jake, 'like a nugget of ice.'

'They must have both belonged to Sylla.' Cal turned them over in her hand.

'Maybe the cold is a warning,' said Jake.

From the darkness came a faint, low, chattering noise, answered with tiny clicks and whirrs.

Cal and Jake froze.

'What's that? Who's there?'

Nothing stirred, but quiet hissing whispers began, growing louder, nearer . . .

They strained to see anything in the black water. Then slowly, all around them, sparks of blue, yellow and green light pricked the dark. One by one, with their luminous lures and flashes, the monstrous creatures of the Serpent's Throat appeared: dragonfish with glassy eyes, devil fish with huge razor-toothed jaws, black sprawling squid.

The lantern fish panicked and fled. Jake lunged just in time to grab one and imprison it in his fist.

Something nipped Cal's fluke. She screamed.

'Get away!' She swung her arms and flicked her tail, raising spinning stones in the swirling water. Jake lashed out with his scraper. In a flash the lights went out. They were left in darkness. The water settled about them.

'Where are you?'

Jake opened his fist slightly. A chink of light escaped from the lantern fish which struggled frantically to swim free. Cal dashed to Jake.

'We're not welcome here,' she said, rubbing her bruised fluke. 'Sylla wouldn't have come to such a dreadful place. How could I have even thought she would? We'll never find the shell.' Cal sank into a dismal mood. 'Hold tight,' she said. 'Don't let the lantern go. If we lose her we'll never leave here alive.'

They swam upwards nervously – feeling before them with every stroke. Their tiny weak light was little more than a comfort. It wasn't strong enough to show them the way. Neither spoke. Then Jake broke the silence.

'I think she's growing dimmer,' he said. 'Is she dying?'

'She's a wild creature. She will die if we keep her. But look!' Cal pointed to a pale glow above them. 'That might be the entrance to Gaping Craw.'

Jake opened his fist and let the lantern fish go free.

'Why did you do that?' gasped Cal. 'If it isn't the way out we'll be—'

'Now we've all got a chance,' interrupted Jake. 'Look, she's swimming that way too. I think you could be right!'

Twenty-nine

Knowledge

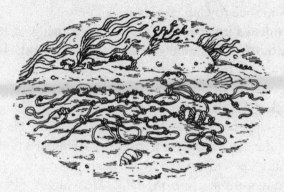

With great relief Cal and Jake emerged from the Serpent's Throat into the cavern of Gaping Craw. Even that weird, haunting place was a welcome sight after the dreadful darkness below.

They swam once more between the columns of light towards the high ledge on the opposite wall. Jake had the wonderful feeling that he was flying through a moonlit cathedral.

Cal was also pleased to be swimming freely again. She threw back her head so that her long hair spread like a sea fan through the water, flashing with coppery lights. She began to wonder what they should do next.

'Do you think Sylla's crystals were warning us we were in the wrong place? Maybe she left them to help us. Maybe *they* will show us the right place to look for the shell, somehow.'

They reached the ledge and the entrance of the narrow passage. Jake tested the metal scraper with his thumb. Not much of a weapon, he thought. He picked up a stone, the size of his fist.

'I'll go first again,' he said and entered the dark crack in the rock.

Jake sidled through the crevice and stepped out into the clearing beyond. He blinked in the brighter light. Then he saw Skimmer's body. Cal was right behind.

'No!' She rushed past him and threw herself across the ray's back. Jake knelt down beside her.

'Is he – has he—' Jake choked on his words. He started to brush the sand frantically from the Skimmer's body.

Cal laid her ear to the ray's heart. 'No,' she gasped, '. . . I don't think . . . oh, Jake. He's alive!' She kissed Skimmer's head. 'Come on, come on. Don't give up. It's me. I'm here now.'

'Bloodfin!' Jake cursed. 'They're not hunters, they're just killers.'

'No, look!' Cal drew her hands across Skimmer's great wings. 'There are no wound marks. The Bloodfin always carry weapons, don't they?'

Jake saw she was right. Then who could have done this? He looked around anxiously.

'Please, help me,' urged Cal. Jake turned from his guard. Together they stroked Skimmer, working in a slow, rhythmical motion, from his head to his wings, over and over again. At last, with great excitement, they felt his muscles stir beneath their hands. Then, to their delight, his gills fluttered and he shuffled from side to side as if waking from a deep sleep, lifted himself a few inches and rippled a short distance away. He turned to face them, and then sank on to the sand once more.

'If only you could tell me what happened,' said Cal a while later. She lay beside Skimmer, continuing to stroke his long wing as he recovered his strength.

Jake was keeping watch. Indistinct shapes moved among the tall fangs of rock around the edge of the clearing. Skimmer had found them, he thought, how long before the Bloodfin did too?

'Why can't you communicate with Skimmer like you do with the others?' he asked.

'He's been like this since my mother died,' explained Cal. 'My father said it's very strange for a creature to say nothing with scent or sound. But we understand each other. I can tell lots from the way he moves – or doesn't!' She kissed his head again. Once more Skimmer stirred. This time he seemed more alert. He fed from the water around.

'So,' Jake sighed. 'When he's strong again where do we start looking for that shell?'

At these words Skimmer stopped feeding and skated across the sand towards Jake, whipping his tail from side to side. He nudged him with his horn.

'Hey!' Jake laughed. 'You're feeling better!'

Skimmer jostled him again, more forcefully this time.

'Hold on,' cried Jake. 'What does he want?'

Cal swam beneath the manta's wing. 'He's excited about something—'

'I just asked about the shell,' said Jake.

'The shell,' said Cal to Skimmer. 'Is that it? Is that what's making you excited?'

Skimmer lifted his wing and took off, wheeling around the clearing. Then he glided low and hovered before them, thumping his tail emphatically.

'What could he know about it?' said Jake. 'Sylla only had the shell before she died . . .' Jake knew he was missing something. 'Wait a minute,' he cried. 'If Sylla was so weak, who brought her to Tarian? Who took her to hide the shell?'

That was it. Skimmer ruffled his wingtips furiously and raised a cloud of sand. He butted Jake gently with his horns and knocked him over!

'Skimmer, was it you?' shrieked Cal. She couldn't believe she hadn't thought of it before. 'Did you carry Sylla? Do you know where she took the shell?'

Skimmer scooped Cal up and rolled her onto his back. 'You knew all along!'

Jake jumped and stamped his feet. 'We've found it! We've found it!' He whooped out loud. 'Wait for me – I'm coming too!'

Skimmer swayed, tipped Jake onto his other wing and took off, heading into the gully. None of them noticed the crumple of twine lying in the sand below – the message Tangler had taken from Skimmer's jaw. The message from Pelin.

Thirty

Breaker

The journey through Fang Gully was a switchback ride. As Skimmer manoeuvred between the towering spines Cal and Jake were flung from side to side. Cal soon slipped off and followed behind, however Jake had no alternative but to grip the rim of Skimmer's wing and hang on with white knuckles. Every roll twisted Jake's arms painfully and swung his legs so close to the sharp rocks that he had to keep pulling up his knees. He was extremely relieved when at last they rose out of the valley.

Skimmer headed into open water. Cal noticed he didn't move with his usual ease. Each time his left wing reached the height of its undulating sweep he winced. She guessed that his muscles were bruised. As he raised his head she also saw a swollen patch at the base of his skull. She moved up to swim next to him.

'You should be resting. I hope we don't have to go far . . .' Skimmer tipped his head towards Cal and gently brushed her cheek with his paddle-shaped horn.

'I'll look out for some balmweed,' said Cal, 'that's good for a swelling.'

The current grew stronger and Skimmer, having to swim against it, made slow progress. Cal looked around for any landmarks that might help to identify where they were heading. After a while the sandbed glowed orange ahead of them.

'It's a farm,' said Cal. 'Sea squirts, look!'

Sure enough they were soon passing over a vast colony of translucent fingers, swaying as they silently siphoned the water.

'How do you know it's a farm?' asked Jake. 'It just looks like a patch of squirts to me.'

'Look at the markers . . .' said Cal.

At first Jake didn't notice anything, then he began to spot clumps of kelp five or six feet tall, bunched together and bound loosely into sheaves. Each binding was threaded with a pair of identical fish bones. When they came to the edge of the squirts there was a further stretch of scarlet feather-stars, then another of purple vase sponges and rippling silkweed. More strands of bound kelp were distributed among them. However, beyond the farm they soon entered featureless, barren waters.

Suddenly a blur of swimming shapes gathered form ahead.

Jake ducked behind Skimmer's wing.

'No, it's all right. They're Silvertails,' said Cal with delight. 'A large pod.' Sure enough Jake saw a group of thirty or more of all ages, heading in the same direction. The pod moved slowly as there were many young and elderly Delphines among them. Several had bundles strapped to their backs and others pulled heavily laden turtle-shell sleds. The young kept to the centre of the group, travelling close to their mothers. Around the outside of the pod swam the older ones, armed with pikes and harpoons. They were accompanied by a flotilla of fish taking advantage of their protection and hoping for scraps of food. As they sensed Skimmer's approach the group turned, uneasy at first, then obviously happy to see one of their own.

'Hide yourself,' whispered Cal to Jake. 'I think they must be fleeing the Bloodfin.' She told Skimmer to hold back and swam ahead to meet them.

Jake crouched on Skimmer's wing, twenty yards away from the group and peeped out cautiously. He watched the Silvertails greet Cal with great fuss and many questions. They pointed back to where they had come from and Jake saw their friendly smiles turn to expressions of anguish. A shy young Silvertail showed Cal spear wounds along her lower body. Another had her arm bandaged with weed. They all began to talk frantically at once. Cal looked worried. She pointed to Skimmer and Jake hid himself from sight.

When Cal returned a short while later there was no sign of the Delphines. They had continued on their way.

'Bloodfins?' Jake guessed.

'Yes. They were collecting oysters in the shallows when a gang caught them,' said Cal. 'The Bloodfin took the oysters and taunted the young one with spears. They threatened to kill them both. But as the mother tried to wrestle with the Bloodfin, so many fish were disturbed close to the surface that a flock of seabirds dived into the water. There was a great commotion and in the confusion they escaped. They managed to get back to warn their pod at Amber Ridge where they live. Now they're all terrified. They've fled from their homes and are too afraid to go back.'

'Where will they go?' asked Jake.

'They're heading for the nearest Bluestreak settlement. Bluestreak Delphines live just beyond our homewaters. But the journey will take many tides at the pace they have to go with the weak ones and the young.'

'What did you tell them?' asked Jake.

'I told them I was sure they'd be able to return soon. I promised them there was hope. The Sea Spirit would not allow the water to run red with this bloodshed.' Cal hesitated. 'They hadn't heard news of my kin-shoal. They hadn't seen any other Silvertails since they left.' She rubbed tears from her eyes and threw herself onto Skimmer's back. 'Come on, Skimmer,' she said, 'I know it hurts, but take us to the shell – *as fast as you can!*'

They had not travelled much further when Skimmer eased out of the strong current and into a warmer, gentler flow. Beneath them the seabed teemed with life once more.

As they journeyed on the warmth of the sea began to puzzle Cal.

'It's curious, this water,' she said.

'It's great,' said Jake, 'almost like a bath.'

'And look at the light – there's something unnatural about it.'

Sure enough the light was brighter now. The water

became crystal clear and sparkled with flecks of emerald and turquoise, as Jake had never seen before.

They swam on, until at last an expanse of rock rose in the distance before them.

'Jake, it's a breaker. Skimmer's heading straight for it. The shell might be there!' Cal immediately raced off towards it.

Jake let go of Skimmer's wing and somersaulted off his back. He raced after Cal.

'What's a breaker?' he called out. He could feel her excitement tingle in the water. But Cal didn't answer. She swam as she had never swum before: her aim so true she hardly needed to move a muscle to trim her course, so fast she barely felt the resistance of the water at all.

Skimmer drifted to the seabed, exhausted from the effort of swimming with his painful wings. The warmth made him drowsy and after a few gulps of the plankton-rich water he settled himself to rest.

'What *is* a breaker?' repeated Jake as he caught up with Cal at the rock wall. She was looking earnestly for shells among the colourful tapestry of coral and anemones that covered every inch of the sloping wall.

'It breaks the surface,' said Cal. 'It's where the seabed rises into the Overbreath.'

Jake looked up through the amazingly clear water. Far above them the wall broke through the surface into the air.

'It's an island!' Jake started to follow the wall to his left and found it curved gently and continued to do so until it returned him to Cal, who was searching with increasing frustration.

'It's an island!' Jake exclaimed.

'Help me look,' urged Cal, without raising her head. 'I

can't see any shells like the one Tarian showed us.'

'I didn't see anything either.' Jake thought for a moment. 'Maybe it's hidden in a cave or something on the island itself?'

An eel swam out of the blue and snaked around Cal's tail. She shook it off impatiently. 'Well, look there if you like,' she said. 'But don't be long. We're close, I can feel it.'

Jake swam up the island slope. A young grey seal shadowed him briefly. Halfway up a shoal of startled scarletinas darted out from the shaggy brown wrack that grew on the higher rock. Moments later, Jake was within reach of the surface that shimmered like crumpled silk above his head. He thrust his arms through it and gasped.

Jake found himself just beyond a rocky cove. He swam slowly around the island once more, looking for a place where Sylla might have hidden her shell. But he found no likely nooks or ledges in the bone-white rock rising from the water. Jake returned to the cove. It seemed to be the only accessible place. He made for the nearest boulder, heaved himself out of the water and clambered from one rock to another on to a tiny pebble beach. There he threw himself on to the shingle to catch his breath and steady his giddy head.

The dazzling sunshine was fierce after the filtered light Jake had grown used to. For a while he could only look into the shadow cast by his body on the ground. A breeze whipped his hunched back. Jake shivered and shook his dripping hair. He felt shockingly raw in the air, naked somehow without the caressing water around him, his limbs heavy and clumsy.

When he had recovered himself Jake stretched his legs. He explored the cove, but found nothing more than blue wings of empty mussel shells and a scattering of limpets. He helped a hermit crab into a shady rock pool.

Hermit Crab

'No point looking inland,' he said to himself. 'Sylla couldn't leave the water.'

But before he turned back to the sea Jake noticed a grassy knoll above the cove. Guessing he might see the whole island from there he decided to climb up to take a look. He was right. From that vantage point Jake saw the full extent of the small island with its bare, bleached rock and patches of scrubby coarse grass. There wasn't a single tree and no neighbouring land within sight. It seemed a lonely place. Good thing too, thought Jake as he suddenly realised that he hadn't even considered the possibility of it being inhabited.

What would I have done if someone had seen me climb out of the sea like that? He explored a little. The crunch of his feet on the rough grass broke the silence of the place. Where were the noisy colonies of gulls he'd expect on a rock like that? There wasn't a bird to be seen, on the ground or in the sky.

'That's odd,' Jake exclaimed aloud. The sound of his voice in the air caught him by surprise. Suddenly he felt out of place, unnerved and desperately alone. He wanted to be back in the sea. He began to walk, then run, tripping and slipping down the slope towards the cliff.

'Cal,' he yelled, 'I'm coming!'

Thirty-one

Cave of Shells

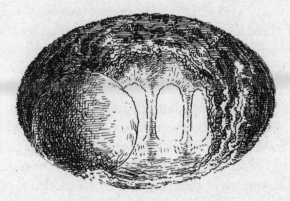

J ake dived to the seabed and searched for Cal along the
breaker wall. She was struggling with a huge boulder,
twice her size, which lay against the rock face. Skimmer
was there too, hovering at her side. Both looked agitated,
but pleased to see him.

'Look!' She pointed to a slip of light escaping from a
gap around the boulder. 'There's something behind this.
Skimmer showed me. Help me push the rock away.' Jake
put his shoulder to it.

'We'll never move this,' he puffed. 'It weighs a ton.'

'We have to,' insisted Cal. 'This is where Skimmer
brought Sylla. There must be a way.' She shoved hard and

157

her pendant swung out and clattered against the rock.

'Oh no!' Cal pulled the necklace over her head to see if the crystal was damaged.

'I wonder . . .' Jake fumbled for the stone in his pocket. 'If this is where we're supposed to look . . .' He took Cal's necklace from her hand and put the two halves of Sylla's stone together. Nothing happened. Jake shrugged apologetically.

'No, wait,' said Cal. She felt the movement of the water around them change. It began to condense into a tight circling current. Round it flowed, gathering strength, swirling about Jake's feet and curling around Cal's tail. As the spinning water rose Cal felt her hair spiral into a twist above her head. Jake's shirt floated up under his armpits and his feet lifted slightly from the ground. The whirlpool grew, drawing in scraps of weed and tiny creatures, spreading wider and wider, until its outer sweep passed across the surface of the boulder. All of a sudden they heard a grinding sound. The boulder began to shift, rolled aside by the force of the water. Then, as quickly as it had gathered, the whirlpool subsided. Jake sank to his feet.

'Now,' urged Cal, 'let's push!' They pushed the huge stone together and it slid smoothly aside, revealing a wide archway. Out of it poured warmth and light.

Jake shut his eyes for a moment and let the balmy wave wash over him, but Cal crossed the threshold eagerly.

Before them was a grotto, with a high vaulted ceiling supported by towering pillars and arches of rock. Suspended from the roof was a hanging garden of coral, feather stars and sea fans, all wafting in a gentle current. Shoals of countless fish drifted through the archways, but they were not like any Jake or Cal had seen before – some had peacock stripes, others were bright as butterflies. It was as if a rainbow had shattered into living splashes of colour and fallen into the sea.

They swam further inside. The warm water cast a spell of harmony. Beneath them clownfish played among vivid anemones. Seadragons fluttered their lacy fins. A pair of parrotfish snapped at a scampering shrimp.

'Look at this,' gasped Jake as he trailed behind Cal. 'Look – look at that!'

But Cal swam beneath the arches silently. As she had hoped, the seabed was scattered with shells – huge green turbans, fretted cowries, triton trumpets and blushing conch. The magnificent molluscs grazed slowly across the coral.

Jake stopped beside a giant clam and stooped to pick up a pearl the size of a hen's egg that lay beside it. He turned it over in his hand. 'What a prize,' he said to himself. A big pearl like that would make him rich. But what would he do with money? 'A trawler full of gold won't buy a cockleshell of happiness,' Lil used to say whenever she saw the folly of rich folk. Jake looked around him. It couldn't buy one glimpse of that enchanted place either. He placed the pearl back beside the clam.

Meanwhile Cal had spotted several nautilus shells.

'Of course,' she said. 'The best place to hide the shell is with others just the same.'

'But it won't be just the same, will it?' said Jake, peering into a blue vase sponge almost as tall as himself. 'The shell Tarian showed us was brightly coloured.'

'Like this one,' said Cal with a sigh, 'and that . . . and those over there . . .'

She fingered her mother's pendant and imagined how Sylla must have felt, weak and dying, reaching this wonderful place. Maybe she never left it . . .

'*Where? Where is the breath?*' she asked silently.

Then Cal felt the pendant begin to grow warmer in her hand. Not just warm with the water, but radiant with heat.

'Jake, your crystal – can you feel it?' Cal turned to Jake behind her, but at once the pendant cooled. She spun away from him and it became warm again. Cal started to swim over the cushions of coral and fat-fingered anemones, following the pendant's lead. Whenever it began to cool she adjusted her direction until it felt warm again. The pendant led her deeper into the grotto.

Jake dashed after Cal, swimming with one arm as he reached into his pocket for his own crystal. But the pocket was twisted.

'Wait for me!' He wriggled his fingers to free the stone, looking down as he did so, and swam straight into a column of rock.

'Ouch!' Jake yelped, rubbing his shoulder. Cal turned and saw Jake's crystal drop out of his pocket and fall toward the seabed. She swooped to catch it. At once, with both stones in her hands, the direction indicated by their warmth was plain. 'There!' she cried. 'I can see it now. I can see the shell!'

Cal pointed. Nestling at the base of a pillar in a patch of olive coral was a nautilus shell, larger than any of the others they had seen. And it was striped with the colours of sunset, just like the one Tarian had shown them.

'We've found it!'

Suddenly a dark streak sped past them, making straight for the shell. A giant conger eel swept down and coiled around the nautilus.

'Get away!' shouted Jake as he and Cal dived forward.

'Stay back. *The shell is mine!*' With horror they recognised the voice of Orcara.

Jake and Cal looked around, but she was nowhere to be seen. Then turbulence began to bubble around the eel. The creature writhed about the shell as if in spasms of pain. To their astonishment, it began to swell, fatter and fatter, until it became a bloated black bladder – so monstrous that its skin started to split. Out burst tangles of squirming, stinking kelp. More spewed forth, and more until the smothering heap gathered itself into the familiar form of Orcara! She parted the weed from her face and thrust a hand to her mouth. To Jake and Cal's disgust she pulled the eel with the V-shaped scar, tail first, from her throat. Orcara cast the eel away and wiped the spittle from her lips. She peered at them with a hideous grin.

For a moment Jake and Cal were too stunned to speak.

Jake broke the silence. 'What . . . what do you want?' He stuttered. 'How did you get here?'

'Your wake has been easy to follow,' Orcara sneered. 'I told you I have many eyes. My reach is far.'

'But why?'

'Can't you guess?' she whined. 'I have waited for you both, waited for countless tides!' She chuckled with amusement at their confused faces. 'You, Creeper-kin, your nauseous birth-scent reached me while you still bleated in your mother's arms. How I rejoiced at the news of your ugly limbs!' She turned her penetrating gaze on Cal. 'And I have hidden close to you, Calypsia, so close that I could have snatched you many times, even from your father's care. But I learnt of your fateflow. Only both together could redeem this prize – my destiny!' She glared with passion at the nautilus lying before her.

'But that's mine!' cried Cal. 'It belonged to my mother.'

'It will *never* belong to you,' snarled Orcara. She bent and picked up the shell. To Cal's disgust she began stroking it. 'This breath is my inheritance!' Orcara threw back her head, flinging venom slugs from her freakish locks, and shrieked with triumph. Every living creature fled from the terrifying sound. The coral shrank. Even the light grew dim.

'Who *are* you?' said Cal.

Orcara swelled and lurched towards her. Sparks flashing from her eyes electrified the water. 'I am Aran,' she said. 'And I will be the Merrow.'

Jake saw Cal fall limply towards the sand. He raced to her side and swung his arm around her.

'Aran?' Cal gasped. 'You mean you're – you're—'

'Yes. I am Sylla's sister.' Orcara exploded with fierce laughter. Then, as if a mask had fallen, her face soured into an ugly scowl. Orcara gazed at the shell, devouring it with her eyes, stroking it with trembling fingers.

'I was the first born,' she said, 'but I was passed over. Your mother was favoured. The soft-minded one, always there with her loathsome, fawning affections.' She pulled the shell deep into her shroud. 'I asked questions. I was hungry to learn. But Sylla cared for nothing. All day she sang, and when she sang everyone listened. I went unheard. Denied.' Orcara made a foul guttural noise and spat into the water. 'So I found other sisters. Sisters scarred by treachery like me, hungry for power. An ambitious, stonehearted sisterhood. And I waited. Waited for what I guessed would be mine. The Merrow breath.'

'You knew about the Merrows?' said Cal, weakly.

'I gathered knowledge,' said Orcara. 'Knowledge is power.'

With a chill Jake remembered where he had heard those words before. He looked behind him at the deserted cavern and saw shades where there had been light.

'Now I know why my father was afraid,' said Cal.

'Your father was a fool,' snapped Orcara. 'He overheard Sylla as she muttered in her delirium but what he learnt only fed his fear. The Sisterhood gathered Merrow knowledge. Whispers of half-remembered legend and cryptic mysteries. Slowly those fragments became promises of power. While Sylla succumbed to weakness I grew strong. Then even those sisters were afraid. Afraid of me, afraid of my intent. Once more I was denied.'

Orcara raised the shell before her. Its fabulous colours were dimmed in her presence. 'The dark wrath spawned in my empty heart. It is I who have stirred up the currents of disruption and discontent. My will set creatures against one another, against their own nature.'

'The Bloodfin . . .' growled Jake.

'Most biddable!' laughed Orcara. 'I drew them to my purpose and sent them to bring you both to me.'

'But we came to Strapkelp ourselves!' cried Cal.

'So it seemed,' said Orcara, 'and how trusting you were! Now, at last, I shall have the Merrow power. The oceans shall feel my revenge.'

'But—' cried Cal, 'how can the breath of the Sea Spirit be used against the ocean?'

Orcara sneered. 'Your foolish mother released the breath. Once its power is within me I shall use it as I wish! The Sea Spirit will be no more than a forgotten legend. The spirit of Aran will flow through the seas.'

Jake had been transfixed by Orcara's words. Now, suddenly he knew he had to act. He flew towards her, reaching for the shell. Like a whiplash Orcara's eel wrapped itself around his ankle and flung him to the sandbed. At once Orcara grabbed a fistful of glass beads from her kelpish hair. Spitting out a charm she scattered the beads before her. To Cal and Jake's astonishment, a wall of crazed green glass rose around her, distorting her grotesque image so that a dozen misshapen hags leered from within. Jake ripped the eel from his ankle and threw himself against the glass, beating vainly with his fists. Cal joined him.

'No!' she screamed. 'No! No! No!!'

Cal's scream resounded through the water and echoed around the cavern, returning as a sweeter, swelling note. As if a spell had been cast, Jake and Cal let their fists fall. The single sound became strong and rich, growing into a chord of notes that began to weave an entrancing, wordless song.

They looked around for the source of the strange, drifting melody, but no singer was to be seen. Then they saw Orcara. She couldn't bear the sound. She had started to thrash from side to side, to beat her bony knuckles against the glass.

'Sylla!' she cried. 'Silence! Curse you, siren!'

All at once Cal knew it too. From somewhere in her deepest memory she recognised her mother's voice. It had a soulful beauty. She turned away from Orcara and lost herself in the song.

Jake, too, was charmed. His terror fell away.

However, as the melancholy song penetrated Orcara's poisoned mind her skull throbbed with pain. To her it was intolerable. She tried to scream above it.

'Silence!' Once more she raised the shell, but in her torment she struggled now. With tremendous effort she lifted it towards her bloodless lips. 'YOU SHALL BE SILENT!' She opened her mouth, the solitary fang poised to puncture the bubble of breath that rose to the rim of the nautilus shell.

Through the fractured glass Cal and Jake watched a dozen tortured Orcaras shudder uncontrollably. Then at last she could stand it no longer. Dropping the nautilus shell she clasped her hands over her ears.

As the shell fell there was a deafening crash. The glass shattered into a thousand pieces, scattering diamond shards though the water, causing lights to flash like an explosion of cold fire.

Shielding themselves, Cal and Jake dashed towards the nautilus, but the huge body of Tangler tumbled out from behind the nearest pillar and grabbed the shell.

Thirty-two

Inheritance

Tangler threw himself at Orcara in the turmoil of sand and splintered glass. He held the shell high like a trophy. Orcara screeched and clawed at him but Tangler wrapped a huge tentacle firmly about her head and slammed another down to pin her wrists to the ground.

For a ghastly moment everything was held in suspension. No one spoke. Nothing moved except the settling sand. As it fell the light grew bright once more and glistened through it.

Cal stared in disbelief at the monstrous sight of Tangler with Orcara, gagged, twitching furiously beneath him. Could he possibly know what was in the nautilus? She had to have it. She had to take a risk.

'That shell—' she hoped the quiver in her voice wouldn't betray her desperation '—there's something inside that belongs to me. Will you let me take it? I don't want the shell. You can keep that.' Cal fixed him with her eyes and made a tiny movement of her tail. Gently she began to glide towards him.

Tangler pulled the nautilus close. He cradled it and rocked from side to side. Now Jake also took a step forward. Tangler shuffled and wrapped his arms more tightly about the shell.

A voice from behind startled them both.

'You've done well.' Tarian swam out from beyond a stand of gigantic sea fans. He passed beneath the arches towards them. The sailfish that had accompanied him before were nowhere to be seen. He approached Tangler. 'Now give me the shell.'

The octopus hesitated for a moment, then unrolled his tentacle and handed the shell to Tarian.

'So here it is,' said Tarian, peering with narrowed eyes at the nautilus. He stroked the bubble with his finger. 'The most precious breath in the ocean. Who wouldn't trade their heart's desire for this?'

'Give it to Cal,' cried Jake. 'You know it belongs to her!' He felt strong, stirred somehow by the song that still echoed in his head. Jake reached down and grabbed a fistful of weed. Using this to protect his hand he picked up a long shard of glass and stabbed it into the water at Tarian.

Tarian shook his head and sighed. 'Once again you heed only your fear,' he said.

'I'm not afraid,' cried Jake, stepping forward. 'I am the Tide Turner!'

Tarian's steely eyes fixed him. 'Yes, boy. You are the Tide

Turner. Of our kind yet not of our kind.' He paused and smiled. 'But I see this means little to you yet. You must listen and learn what your destiny shall be. Show your courage and trust me now.'

Cal pushed the glass spike from Jake's hand.

'Listen to him,' she said.

Tarian carefully placed the shell down in the coral. Then he turned to Cal.

'When your mother came to me, long ago, I gave her the vessel she wanted without question. But there were mysteries in her eyes that intrigued me. Then I found you searching too, Calypsia, and I saw those same secrets once more. Like Sylla you revealed nothing, except your need for help, and it seemed to me the one you had found knew no more than I did of the fatestream that carried you both. After you left I sent Tangler to follow you, to protect you, while I went to search for the sense of what I'd seen. I travelled fast and far, trading dearly for knowledge. At last the meaning of that prophecy in which we are all destined to play a part became clear to me.'

'I don't understand,' said Cal.

'No.' Tarian nodded. 'But now it is my part to open your eyes. I came swiftly and found your markers at Fang Gully. The sailfish picked up Tangler's scent. They brought me here.'

Jake looked around for the sailfish.

Tarian noticed his frown and smiled. He raised his hand, opening his fingers wide for three yellow damselfish to shimmy through.

'I couldn't trust them around these delicacies!' he said.

A sudden thud from Tangler made them all turn. The octopus brandished Orcara's writhing eel above his head.

'Let me have him!' cried Jake, but Tangler lashed the conger hard by its tail, like a whip. At once the eel stopped jerking. Its snapping jaw fell open and it hung, lifeless. Tangler cast it away.

'Now, heed my words,' said Tarian, 'and understand. In the beginning, at the Great Welling, when the still water was roused to motion by the first wave, the Sea Spirit made all living creatures. These creatures roamed the oceans freely. But, in time, some became curious about what lay beyond, what girdled our world. They were drawn to the unknown. Dissatisfaction grew. Their curiosity became insatiable until the boldest left the sea to live there, in the Overbreath.

That angered the Sea Spirit. She crashed great waves upon the shore. She flooded the land, gathered the sea to rise into the Overbreath and rain down upon it. But she had no power to bring back those who had left. She was afraid that others might follow, that all creatures might turn from the sea. So she created the Merrows – to whom she gave the breath of her own wisdom and power. She charged them with the care and protection of the ocean. Through them the balance of creation was restored and currents flowed in harmony once more. However, if any were ever tempted to turn from the ocean again, the Merrows were to use their powers to bring them back to the ways of the sea.'

'Were there many of them?' asked Cal.

'There were many,' replied Tarian. 'The Merrow breath was passed from mother to daughter through generations. But they were not all blessed with a female child. Over time their number dwindled and now few are left.'

'You mean there are still others?' said Cal in surprise. 'So Sylla was wrong. She was not the last?'

'No, she was not the last,' said Tarian. 'But the oceans are wide.' He picked up a mottled cowrie and rubbed his thumb across its surface. 'We call these waters home, but the Sea Spirit has realms far beyond ours – as many oceans as the dapples on this shell. The protection of the few Merrows that remained was frail. Your mother knew the time of peril, foretold in the prophecy of the Tide Turner, was coming.' He turned to Jake. 'That is why she hid the breath for safekeeping. She invested you with what powers she could and set a whisper upon the water that the Tide Turner would come soon. It was a warning to those who might stir up disruption.'

'Like the Bloodfin?' said Jake.

'Yes,' said Tarian. 'But their wrath has been nurtured by the kelp hag . . .' He glared at Orcara. Her muzzled head, clasped in a great tentacle, jerked furiously. She struggled in vain. Tarian picked up the nautilus and held it out to Cal.

'Take it. Accept your inheritance. Accept your destiny.' He turned to Jake. 'The Sea Spirit needs you both.'

Thirty-three

A Shadow Falls

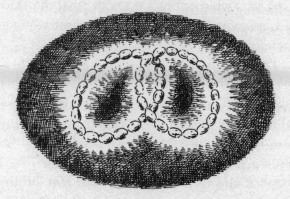

Cal raised the nautilus shell to her lips and drank in the Merrow breath. A sensation of great joy overwhelmed her. She dropped the empty shell and swayed, dizzy with delight. The sea took her weight and lifted her.

Watching, Jake had the uneasy feeling that Cal was somewhere else, beyond his reach. She seemed to have lost all awareness of time and place.

Cal floated before them. The water embraced her, alive with Sylla's presence. She heard the whisper of her mother's voice. Cal felt deeply happy, as though she had remembered something truly wonderful that she'd forgotten long, long ago. Something that made everything right. Something that made everything good. The half shadow which had always been there fell away – and she understood who she was, what she was destined to be. At last she felt peaceful, complete.

'I see now,' she murmured. 'I know what I must do.' Then Cal came to. She rolled over and began to swim slowly, as if in a daze, then gaining strength until she flew among the pillars, flinging her arms like a dancer in the air. At last she slowed and came to rest before Tarian.

'Will you help me now?' she asked.

Doubt fell across Tarian's face. 'I have tried.' He gestured towards Tangler. 'I sent him to protect you, but he misjudged the ray for a threat.' At these words Jake realised that Skimmer had not followed them inside the breaker. But Cal seemed untroubled. 'I will need your help,' she said. Tarian nodded solemnly and bowed his head.

Cal smiled and turned to Jake. 'And you, brother?' she said.

'I don't know,' Jake said, 'I'm still not sure what it all means.'

Cal took his hands. Her emerald eyes shone. 'Sylla had to give you up to the Overbreath, Jake, but you came back. You unlocked the Merrow secret. You are the Tide Turner. Now, together we can redeem the rebellious ones who gathered while the breath was hidden. You belong here, Jake, but I cannot make you stay . . .'

She moved away as if to give him space to consider her words.

Jake hesitated. 'Do I have to choose, now?' he asked. Cal said nothing. In the silence her words took root in his mind. Jake thought of Charley and Lil. He thought of the island so close above him. He looked round at the Delphine world, at his sister – still strange yet familiar to him now. She was the only family he had. But something was missing, he thought. There was something more to belonging . . .

'If only she was here,' he said. 'If only—' The dream of his mother flooded his mind. This time she didn't appear in a watery heaven above, but close before him. He saw clearly her silver hair, tumbling in curls like his own. She raised her pale arms and held out her small, fine hands to him. As she gazed at Jake her smile answered every question in his heart. Then she spoke.

'Come to us,' she said. 'Come to me.' Now Jake knew her voice – not from his dreams, but beyond. From the time when she had been all that was about him. Beyond the dream. In the bright water.

'I'll stay,' he said. 'I *want* to stay!' The vision melted and Jake felt a burst of great happiness. He began to laugh, although he didn't know why. Cal laughed with him. Even Tarian shook his head and smiled.

'So be it,' he said.

Tangler suddenly stirred and kicked a squirm of venom slugs out from beneath his belly.

'What about her?' Jake pointed to Orcara.

Before they could think further the water started to grow much warmer. The rock rumbled beneath them and a shower of tiny molluscs fell from the pillars nearby. Cracks appeared in the seabed around Tangler.

Cal, Jake and Tarian retreated. The water became hot and a chasm opened before them, belching smoke and great bubbles of air. The pillars and arches shook. Rubble and broken coral fell from the roof above.

'Save yourself,' cried Tarian as the octopus clung to Orcara with fright. At once he scrambled off her and fled. As he released Orcara a jet of steam blasted from the chasm. She let out an ear-splitting scream. The kelp was ripped from her body and flung in shreds about her. Orcara vanished in the boiling turbulence. The water swirled about them, dense with hot, stinging sand. Jake wrapped himself around Cal, protecting her from the blast. Then, just as suddenly as it had cracked apart the vent in the rock crumbled upon itself and closed up. To everyone's relief the water cooled quickly and the debris began to settle.

Jake and Cal coughed and spluttered. Their hot faces throbbed and their eyes smarted, but they hardly noticed as the water cleared and the figure of Orcara appeared before them; a grotesque statue, white as bone and shorn of her kelpish shroud, her body petrified in a frozen moment of horror. Her face grimaced and her arms reached up like branches of dead coral.

'She would have cast the waters red with blood,' said Tarian. 'Now she has been denied by the Sea Spirit herself.'

Jake and Cal could only stare, speechless, at the sight. Once more the water became crystal clear and rippling lights played through it.

A blue velvet goby settled on Orcara's finger and five tiny angelfish swam like a circlet around her head. An

Turtle

inquisitive young turtle descended from the roof garden high above their heads, paddling down to see what had caused such a stir. The grotto became busy again, almost as if nothing had happened. Cal found herself crying. Something dropped into her hands and she looked up.

'Skimmer!' He swooped down out of the brilliant blue. Cal and Jake stroked his white belly as he swept over their heads and came to rest beside them.

'Where have you been?' Cal ran her fingers down his head. There was the bruise that Tangler had inflicted. She passed her hand over it and as she did so felt the wound drawn from his flesh into the water. When she removed her hand the dark patch had disappeared.

'Look, Jake. The bruise is gone. I held my hand close and . . . I healed him!' Skimmer rubbed his head against her gratefully then nudged the twine message she had let fall onto the sand; the message he'd returned to Fang Gully to find.

'What have you brought me?' Cal fingered the small mat of woven twine, ragged with plaits and beaded threads. She touched each knot in the sequence carefully. Jake saw her face grow pale.

'What's the matter? What's happened?' he said.

Cal clutched the message. 'It's from my father. Skimmer found him.' For a moment she couldn't speak.

'He's alive?' asked Jake. 'He escaped the Bloodfin?'

'Yes! He was away when they attacked the village – looking for me! He's waiting at Blue Caves. Oh, Jake, he's alive!' Cal realised everything might be all right. No, everything *would* be all right. She had so many questions, so much to tell him. There'd be no secrets now.

Tarian pulled two bracelets of amber beads from his wrist

and handed one each to Jake and Cal. 'Send these when you need me.' He nodded to Jake. 'Look after your sister.'

Jake gripped Tarian's strong hand. 'I was wrong about you,' he said. 'I'm sorry.'

'I'll trade your doubt for friendship,' said Tarian. 'Now go. There is much to be done.'

'Come on!' Jake pulled Cal towards Skimmer, who hovered above them.

Cal took one last look at the grotto, hardly believing what had taken place there. She steadied herself. Whatever lay ahead she was ready for it. She was born for it. Cal thanked Tarian. Then, with the amber bracelet on her wrist and Sylla's pendant around her neck, she reached for Skimmer's wing. 'Let's go home, Jake,' she said. 'I'm going to take you home.'